THE PLANET OF DEATH

When Morgan Chane returned to Varna, planet of his birth, home planet of the star-plundering Starwolves, he saw the neat squadrons of needle-shaped spaceships glinting in the golden sunshine at Krak starport. Varna was as it had always been.

Only it was not. . . .

Chane felt wary and cold. He had left Varna because he had killed one of the Starwolves in a fight, and now that man's entire clan was sworn to kill him. The Starwolves were deadly, and relentless . . . Chane must forget emotions like nostalgia if he was to live.

But if he could carry out his plan, the gamble would be worthwhile. For Morgan Chane intended to steal the most fabulous treasure-hoard in the galaxy, and for that he needed the help of the feared Starwolves. . . .

WORLD OF THE STARWOLVES is the third in Edmond Hamilton's exciting new series of stellar adventures featuring Morgan Chane, the Starwolf. See page 159 for information on the first two Starwolf novels, THE WEAPON FROM BEYOND and THE CLOSED WORLDS.

EDMOND HAMILTON
WORLD OF THE STARWOLVES

STARWOLF #3

ACE BOOKS, INC.
1120 Avenue of the Americas
New York, N.Y. 10036

WORLD OF THE STARWOLVES

Copyright ©, 1968, by Ace Books, Inc.

All Rights Reserved

I

HE WAS a long way now from the stars, and that was all right with him.

Damn the stars, thought Dilullo. *I've had enough of them.*

He sat on the browned, sun-warmed grass on the side of the low hill, hunched with his knees drawn up, looking in his gray coverall like an old rock set in the slope. And Dilullo's face had something rock-like in it too, a roughly carved face of harsh planes, his hair graying at the edges.

He looked down at the streets and buildings of Brindisi, at the cape and the mole and the little islands, with beyond them the blue Adriatic shimmering in the hot Italian sun. He knew the old city very well, but it had changed since he had hurried through it as a boy on his way to school.

Working and studying, to get to be a starman, he thought. *And what did the stars give me when I got to them? Danger and worry and sweat, and when I went out to them once too often I came back to find that everybody and everything I had was gone.*

The sun wheeled lower, and still Dilullo sat and

stared and remembered. Then he was drawn back to the present by the sight of a man walking up the slope toward him.

He was a young man, compact of figure, his dark head bare. He wore a coverall, and there was something about the easy springiness with which he came up the slope that made Dilullo peer more closely. He had never seen but one man who walked quite that way.

"I'll be damned," he said aloud. "Morgan Chane."

Chane came up to him and nodded. "Hello, John."

"What the devil are you doing here?" demanded Dilullo. "I thought you'd have been long gone from Earth on some Merc job by now."

Chane shrugged. "I would have been, only it seems nobody wants to hire Mercs right now."

Dilullo nodded understandingly. The Mercs . . . the Mercenaries . . . would do tough, dangerous jobs anywhere in the galaxy if the pay was right. But sometimes there just weren't any jobs.

"Well, you got enough money for our job at Arkuu to keep you for a while," he said.

Chane smiled. He smiled easily, and his dark, lean face was that of a very nice young Earthman . . . only Dilullo knew that he was not a nice young Earthman at all but a human tiger.

"I thought," Chane said, "that I'd see how your new house is coming along. Where is it?"

"I haven't started building it yet," said Dilullo.

"Not started?" exclaimed Chane. "Why, it's been weeks and weeks since you quite the Mercs and left us. You didn't talk about anything but this grand new house, and how anxious you were to get it started."

"Listen," said Dilullo testily, "if you're going to spend

a lot of money on a house to live the rest of your life in, you don't hurry it too much. You've got to be sure of the right site, the right design . . ."

He broke off and then said, "Ah, what's the use of trying to explain it to you. . . . what does a home mean to a damned Starwolf!"

Chane said, "I'd just as lief you didn't call me that, John. They still hang Starwolves most places if they catch them."

"Don't worry," Dilullo said sourly. "I've never breathed it to a soul. I can well imagine you don't want it told around."

The Starwolves were the natives of a distant heavy planet named Varna, and there was a reason why they were hated and feared all over the galaxy. They were the most competent robbers of all time. Their heavy world had given them unmatchable strength and speed and ability to endure acceleration, and nobody could beat them in space. They had used that advantage to take loot from all over the universe.

Nobody but Dilullo knew that Chane had been a Starwolf. He looked like any other Earthman, and his parents had been Earth folk, but Chane himself was born on Varna and had grown to Varnan strength. He had robbed and roved with the Starwolf squadrons until a quarrel with a comrade had resulted in a fight, and a dead Varnan, and Chane fleeing into exile to avoid the vengeance of the dead man's clan. *And I had to pick him up,* thought Dilullo, *and turn him into a Merc, and he's been a damned good one, but all the same I'm glad I don't have the responsibility for this tiger on my hands anymore.*

Dilullo stood up. "Come on, Chane. I'll buy you a drink."

They went down the slope and into the streets of the old town, and presently sat in a cool, shadowy tavern in which time seemed to have stopped a long while ago. Dilullo ordered, and a waiter brought two bottles, and he shoved one of them across the table.

"Orvieto abboccato," said Dilullo. "The best wine in the whole galaxy."

"If it's that good," said Chane, "why are you drinking whiskey?"

Dilullo answered, a little embarrassed, "The truth is, I've been away from here so long I'm not used to wine any more. It upsets my stomach."

Chane grinned, and drank his wine, and looked around, at the old wooden furniture, at the smoke-blackened ceiling, at the open doorway outside which twilight was coming to the street.

"It's a nice town," said Chane. "A real nice place for a man to retire and live quiet in."

Dilullo said nothing. Chane poured himself more wine and said, "You know, you're lucky, John. When the rest of us are out there beating up the starways, in trouble up to our necks on some faraway planet, why, you'll be sitting here and drinking and taking it easy, real peaceful-like."

He drank and set his glass down and added, "I'd sure like to settle down in a place like this myself when I get old."

"Chane," said Dilullo, "let me give you a bit of advice. Never try to needle people, to cat-and-mouse with them. You don't know how, as you're not quite all human yourself. Now say what you want to say."

"All right," said Chane. He poured more of the straw-colored wine for himself. "John, do you remember that when we came back from Arkuu, we heard the Singing Suns had been stolen?"

"I'm not likely to forget it," said Dilullo. "The greatest art-treasure in the galaxy robbed away by the Starwolves. You must have been real proud of your people."

"I was," said Chane. "Just six ships, slipping in to the throne-world of Achernar and snatching the Suns out from under their noses. Achernar has been screaming bloody murder ever since."

They had, Dilullo knew, and he didn't blame them. The Singing Suns had been their almost-sacred treasure.

They were not really suns. They were synthetic jewels, created long ago by a master craftsman, and the secret of their creation had died with them. Big, varicolored, glorious, the jewels represented the forty biggest stars of the galaxy, revolving in a mobile. And the jewels sang, each one differently . . . the deep and somber note of Betelgeuse, the soaring sweet tone of Altair, the thrilling sounds of Rigel and Aldebaran and Canopus and all the others, blending together into a true music of the spheres.

Chane was still smiling. "They talked of sending a war-fleet to Varna to get the Suns back. But that couldn't be done, for all the independent systems in Argo Spur, where Varna is, wouldn't let their sovereign space be violated by a fleet going through them."

"I've said before," said Dilullo disgustedly, "that it's a damned immoral arrangement. Those Argo systems protect the Starwolves from attack because they profit from the Starwolf loot."

Chane shrugged. "Anyway, the government of Achernar, as a last resort, has offered a two million credit reward to anyone who'll go in there and bring back the Singing Suns."

Dilullo made a harsh sound that was not quite laughter. "They'll get far with that! Who is there in the whole galaxy that's going to try to recover Starwolf loot?"

"I thought some of us might," said Chane.

Dilullo stared at him. He seemed completely serious, but with Chane you never knew.

"Go to Varna? Take something away from the Starwolves? There are easier methods of suicide!"

"The Suns aren't at Varna, John," said Chane. "Do you think the Varnans would just keep them and admire their beauty? I know the Starwolves, and I can tell you they don't care a tinker's damn about art, no matter how great. No, they'd break up the Suns, sell the jewels separately in the thieves' market worlds of Argo Spur."

"Break them up?" exclaimed Dilullo. "Of all the vandalistic, blasphemous things ever heard of. . . ."

Chane shrugged again. "That's what they'd do, John. A thousand to one, the Suns are right now on certain worlds of the Spur. We figure we could get hold of them and claim that two million."

"Who are 'we'?" demanded Dilullo.

"Why, Bollard and Janssen and some of the others have agreed to give it a try," said Chane.

"How did you convince *them* where the Suns are?" said Dilullo. "You couldn't tell them about your Starwolf past."

"I just lied to them," Chane said shamelessly. "I told them I grew up in the Spur and knew a lot about its worlds." He added, grinning, "And so I do, too . . . but from going with the Varnans to barter our loot."

Dilullo was too used to Chane's lack of conventional morality to be surprised. He said, "That Spur is murder. There are more nonhuman- than human-peopled worlds in it, and on nearly all of them you can get killed just for the clothes you're wearing. Supposing that you can locate the Singing Suns there—"

"I can locate them," Chane said. "I know just where loot like that would be sold."

"So you locate them," Dilullo finished, "then how do you figure to get hold of them?"

"Take them," said Chane.

"Just like that? Good old-fashioned Starwolf stealing?"

Chane smiled. "This wouldn't be stealing, John. You forget that the Singing Suns rightfully and legally belong to Achernar, and whoever has them knows it. If we get hold of them, by cunning or force, we're only recovering stolen property for the owners. All legal and honest."

Dilullo shook his head. "Legally, you're right. Even ethically, you're right. But I don't want to hear a Starwolf talking about honesty!"

He added, "Anyway, how do you and Bollard and the rest figure even to get to the Spur? It takes money for an expedition like that, and nobody would advance you a nickel on a venture into that hellhole."

"We all have some money from our Arkuu job," said Chane. "And that's where you come in, John."

"I do, do I? In what way?"

Chane explained brightly, "You got a hundred thousand for your share of that last job. You could help finance this one and take a leader's share if we make it."

Dilullo looked at him across the table for a long time before he spoke.

"Chane," he said, "you're a marvel in one way. You have the most brass of anyone in the universe. You know bloody well that hundred thousand is for my house."

"I didn't figure you would ever build that house," said Chane.

"Why did you figure that way?" asked Dilullo, his voice dangerously soft.

"Because," said Chane, "you don't really want a house. Why have you sat around here for weeks without starting one? Because you know that when the first nail goes into the house it's going to nail you down here and you'll never see the stars again. That's why you've put it off and put it off. I knew you would."

There was a long silence, and Dilullo looked at Chane with a look that Chane had never seen before. Chane tensed himself, ready to spring back out of the way if Dilullo struck at him.

Nothing happened. Nothing except that Dilullo's face became slowly bleaker and that a haggardness came into it. He picked up his glass and drained it and set it down.

"That's a bad thing for you to say to me, Chane," he said. "And the reason it's so bad is that it's true."

He stared down into the empty glass. "I thought it would all be the same here, but it hasn't been. Not at all."

He sat staring into the glass and the lines in his hard face were deep. Finally he stood up.

"Come along," he said.

They went out of the tavern. It was dark, but the moon was bright on the streets of old white buildings.

Dilullo led the way, along a street that went twisting out of town, with the whisper of the sea vaguely audible on their left. Dilullo walked with his shoulders sagging like those of an old man, and he neither looked at Chane nor spoke to him. He finally stopped and stood staring at nothing . . . nothing but a vacant lot between two old stucco houses. He stared silently for a long time.

"This is where my first house was," he said.

Chane said nothing. There was nothing to say. He knew all about that house and how, long ago, Dilullo's wife and children had perished in its burning.

Dilullo suddenly turned and grasped Chane by the arm, so fiercely that even Chane's iron Starwolf muscles felt it.

"I'll tell you something, Chane," he said. "Don't ever go back and try to live things over again. Don't ever do it!"

Then he dropped Chane's arm and turned away. "Ah, let's get the hell out of this place," he said. "Let's go to the Argo Spur."

II

THE GALAXY wheeled through infinity, a vast, spinning, lens-shaped storm of stars. Out from its central mass trailed mighty spirals, and one of these spirals was isolated, sweeping far out into space. It had a dim, tarnished look compared to the other vast arms of the galaxy, for beside its myriad suns this spiral contained many dark nebulae and an unusual number of dead stars. It was often called the Dark Spiral, but its other name was the Argo Spur.

Beauty and horror, riches and danger, worlds of men and many more worlds of not-men, were in the Dark Spiral. None knew that better than Morgan Chane, as he sat in the bridge of the little speeding ship and looked and looked, his face dark and brooding. What he looked at in the viewscreen was not an actuality but an accurate simulacrum, for they were in over-drive and in non-space direct vision is impossible.

The fabric of the ship was shuddering and shaking around him. It was an old ship and its overdrive was not very good. It did what it was supposed to do, it hurled them across extra-dimensional space toward the spiral at its highest speed, but it trembled and creaked ominously all the time it did so.

Chane disregarded that. He looked at the spiral in the simulacrum and his eyes were fixed on a tawny yellow star blazing deep in the wilderness of the Argo Spur.

And how often I've come this way, he thought.

The superb tawny-gold sun was the primary of the planet Varna, the most hated world in the galaxy.

And this vast, far-flung spiral of stars ahead was the old road of the Starwolves. Through it they had come and gone on their way to raid the systems of the main part of the galaxy. And through it Chane had come and gone with them, so that there was little about the tangle of suns and dead stars and dark nebulae that he did not know at least something about.

The little ship hurtled on, still trembling and whispering uneasily. There was nothing for a pilot to do when a ship was in overdrive. All that was needed was a man in the bridge to keep watch on the telltales of the overdrive units. Chane was the man now, and he did not at all like the way the telltales quivered.

After a time, Bollard came into the bridge. He looked at the instruments and shook his head.

"This ship is a dog," he said. "A worn-out old dog."

Chane shrugged. "It's the best we could lease for the kind of money we had."

Bollard grunted. He was a fat man, so fat that his paunch bulged out his coverall, and he had a moon-like face with crinkles around his eyes. He looked slobbish, but Chane, who had been out twice with him, knew that Bollard was strong and fast and tough, and that in a fight he was about as slobbish as a sword-blade.

Bollard touched a switch, and a simplified star-chart was projected into being. He looked at the blip of their ship, now well into the base of the spiral.

"You said you had an idea about where we'd drop out of overdrive," he said to Chane. "Where?"

Chane indicated with his finger a small area marked in red.

"There."

Bollar stared. "That's a Zone 3 danger area. Do we *have* to go into it?"

"Look," said Chane, "we've been all over that. We'll be scanned from the time we enter the Spur and we've got to look like the drift-miners we're supposed to be, which means that we have to go where drift-miners would go."

"We could skirt around the area and make like we are mining without going into it," said Bollard.

Chane smiled. "That's a real clever idea. Only, when we get to Mruun, we've got to show some reason for coming there, and some valuable ores to sell would be a good reason."

Bollard seemed unconvinced, and Chane added,

"You don't know the Spur. I do, for, as I told you, my parents were Earth missionaries who moved from one of the Spur systems to another when I was growing up . . ."

He thought that the first part of his statement was true, even though the rest was not. His parents had indeed been dedicated missionaries, but Varna alone had been the scene of their mission, and they had lived and worked and failed and finally died on Varna.

". . . and I can tell you," Chane finished, "that on some of the Spur worlds, just one whisper, one breath, of suspicion will get you killed quick."

"I still don't like this idea," grumbled Bollard. "It's all very well for you; you were a drift-miner before you joined the Mercs. But I've never been a rock-hopper."

Chane said nothing. He had told them he was a drift-miner to cover up his Starwolf past, but he had never been one and he thought he had a tricky time ahead of him.

He thought it even more when, finally, the blip of their creaking ship had moved quite near to the red patch of the danger area. Dilullo, sitting in the co-pilot chair beside Chane, studied the chart.

"We'd better drop out of overdrive here," he said.

"We can go a little closer," Chane said.

They went closer, and Dilullo began to fidget. Presently he said decisively, "That's close enough. Drop out."

Chane shrugged, but obeyed. He pressed a button that gave the alert signal throughout the ship, and set up the controls.

Chane moved a switch, and they dropped out. And Chane, who had done this hundreds of times, thought again that it was something like dying and then being born again. From the extra-dimensional space in which they had been traveling, he seemed to fall through vertiginous abysses. Every atom in Chane's body felt shock, his senses whirled, and then they came out of it.

And now the viewscreens no longer presented a simulacrum. The glory of the Argo Spur was revealed and there smashed in upon them the light of ten thousand suns.

A series of ear-piercing shrieks came from the drift indicators. At the same instant, Chane saw great and small bulks hurtling by the ship.

"*Knew* we were getting too close!" yelled Dilullo.

Chane saw death looking him in the eye. Their little ship had dropped into space right inside a colossal stream of stone and metal. And they couldn't go back into overdrive until the unit recycled.

"This damned drift has changed since I last saw it!" he exclaimed. "Sound the hooter!"

Dilullo pulled a lever and the hooter alarm yelled stridently through the ship.

An odd-shaped mass of stone was bearing down on them. Chane hit the controls and stood the ship on its tail. There was a rattling of tiny particles on the hull and he hoped they weren't holed. Dilullo was shouting something, but between the hooter and the constant shrieking of the drift-alarms he couldn't hear what it was.

Radar and sight both informed him of another weird-shaped mass coming at them, tumbling over and over. He hit the controls again.

Then the Starwolf surged up in Chane. They were trapped in this bloody cataract of drift and they probably weren't going to get out of it alive, and all the

17

careful maneuvering in the world wouldn't do them any good now. He took the Varnan way, the way he and his old comrades would have taken had they been in a bind like this. He held steady on the steering and smashed his free hand down on the power and sent the ship hurtling blindly ahead at full normal speed.

Gamble your ship and your life. It was better than trying useless dodgings and turnings and getting killed anyway.

Chane's teeth showed in a mirthless smile. He had had a good life as long as it lasted, and if it had to end he was not going to claw like a frightened old woman against the inevitable. No.

Dilullo was still yelling at him, but he paid no attention. John was a good man but he wasn't a Starwolf, and he was getting a mite old.

A monstrous face of stone whirled past them. A face with bunches of tentacles instead of eyes, and a protuberant trunk-like mouth, and nothing human about it.

The ship slammed through particle-drift again, and past another face that had no relation to humanity, and then past a mighty tumbling statue of a thing with the same tentacle-eyed face and too many arms and legs.

Faces, figures, a phantasmagoria of nightmare shapes . . . and of a sudden the scream of the drift-alarms shut off. They were out of the cataract of meteoric drive and into clear space.

Chane took a long breath. The gamble did pay off, sometimes. He turned around and looked at Dilullo with a bright smile.

"What do you know?" he said. "We made it."

Dilullo started to curse deeply. Then he shut it off.

"All right, Chane," he said. "I thought we had taken some of that Varnan out of you. I see we didn't. I'll remember that."

Chane shrugged. "You've got to admit, it was no place to hang around in."

Dilullo said, "Those faces . . . those figures. What the devil is this place?"

"Some sort of nonhuman cemetery, I think," said Chane. "Long before there were ever men in the Spur, there were other races. They made meteors into memorials."

"Nobody's ever mined this drift," Chane explained. "At least I don't think so. You see, everybody's superstitious about it. I figured this would be the best place to pick up some precious ores, before we head for Mruun."

Dilullo shook his head. "I might have known it. Robbing a galactic graveyard. Only a Starwolf would think of that!"

III

CHANE, in his spacesuit, cuddled up against the gigantic, unhuman stone face and prepared to commit mayhem upon it. His analyzer had told him there was a rich palladium ore-pocket in this sculptured shard of stone. He thought, from his readings, that if he cut out the ear of the thing he could easily reach it.

Stars above, around, and below him, the bright pitiless face of infinity. The great river of stones, some of them sculptured in awesomely alien busts, others stark and untouched, flowed serenely on through the void. These meteors and broken asteroids moved at the same pace but they did change position in regard to each other, so that one had to be wary of a bulk of stone slowly and majestically approaching and grinding one to powder.

Clinging like a fly to the monstrous face, Chane hauled around the ato-torch that hung from a sling hooked to his suit. It fouled with the sling of the analyzer and he tugged at it impatiently.

"Chane!"

The voice came from the receiver in his helmet, and it was the voice of Van Fossan.

"Chane, you're not going to cut into one of the heads? Remember John's orders."

Chane muttered a curse under his breath as he turned and saw the spacesuited figure angling toward him, using an impeller to drive himself forward. Van Fossan was a young and eager-beaver Merc, and he would show up just at this time.

Chane remembered very well what Dilullo's orders were. Before they left the ship, which was now cruising outside the meteor stream and keeping pace with it, Dilullo had said, "The people or not-people who carved those heads have been gone a long time. But a memorial is a memorial. I wouldn't want strangers prospecting for ore in my tombstone, and neither would you. Leave them alone."

Chane had made no objection to what he considered Dilullo's sentimentality. But he had never meant to be bound by it. It was his bad luck that Van Fossan had come up on him.

"I just stopped to untangle my slings," Chane said. "You go on ahead."

He waited until Van Fossan had gone, a small figure

against the backdrop of an infinity of suns, angling away across the majestically flowing river of stones.

When he was out of sight, Chane unshipped his cutting laser and began to slice into the edge of the monstrous ear.

"*Stranger . . .*"

Chane stiffened, his head swiveling, his eyes glaring around him for the one who had spoken.

"*Stranger, spare us our pitiful immortality. . . .*" Chane suddenly realized that the words were reaching his mind, not his ears, and that they were not words at all but thoughts. Telepathic speech. "*If you are here at all, you are a lord of the starways. We were lords of the starways . . . and of all our might and magnificence only these stone faces are left. Leave us this much. . . .*"

Chane rebounded with a galvanic kick of his feet from the huge stone head. He floated near it, and then he laughed.

So that's why these heads have never been mined, he thought; *a telepathic record set in each one.*

He told himself that both superstition and sentimental appeals were lost on him; but if the telepathic bit still worked, there might well be other and nastier things about the monuments that still worked.

Chane switched on his impellers and went away from there. He angled through a shoal of fine drift, feeling it rattle like hail against his tough suit and helmet. The light of the Argo suns glanced down on him, and by it he saw other Mercs in the distance, swimming like dark men-fish amid the drift, searching and going on and pausing to search again.

He too swam and stopped and searched and searched again, using the analyzer. It told him nothing. He began to get irritated by his failure. It seemed to him that the eyeless stone faces sneered at him as they went by.

A queer uneasiness came upon Chane. For a time he did not understand what caused it. Then he remembered. The last time he had moved like this, in his spacesuit, alone in the drift, it had almost been his death. He had been wounded, exhausted, with the Starwolves hunting him, and he had seemed to float all solitary in the universe with the bright eyes of the suns of Corvus Cluster pitilessly watching him. Only the fact that his signal had brought Dilullo's Merc ship had saved him.

"To the devil with it," Chane muttered to himself. "That's past history."

He forced himself to shrug off the feeling, to get on with his job, to impel himself deeper into the drift, keeping clear of jagged meteors and unhuman stone faces that bore down upon him. But wherever he pointed his analyzer, it seemed that there was nothing any good.

"Chane," said Dilullo's voice inside his helmet, startling him.

"Yes?"

"Return to ship."

"John, I haven't got hardly a thing," said Chane.

"The others have," answered Dilullo. "Come on back."

Chane, as he forsook the seach and cut in his impeller to highest power, was not sorry to lift up out of the majestic never-ending parade of stone faces that moved forever through the drift.

As he shot in front of one of the great faces that was bearing down on him, he turned and made a disrespectful sound toward it.

In the hold of the ship, he put down the small chunks of ores he had brought along in his net carrier.

"You got less than any of us!" Sekkinen said loudly to him. "You, the professional rock-hopper."

Sekkinen was a tall, rawboned man who had the habit of saying emphatically just what he thought. He did not much like Chane.

Chane shrugged. "You just had beginners' luck. I didn't. That's the way it goes."

He looked around at the haul, glistening chunks of stone and metal, frosty with the utter cold of infinity.

"It's not very much," he said.

"A good chunk of terbium, some palladium, and a few of the rare C-20 ores," said Dilullo. "No, it doesn't amount to much. But we'll get more as we go on."

They went on. The little ship crept perilously along the coast of one of the dark nebulae that dimmed the Argo Spur. Its main analyzer probed ahead, seeking treasure. Nothing.

They crept on and on, still coasting that enormous cloud. Finally there came a time when Bollard, who handled the big analyzer, said sourly, "I've got it . . . but you won't like it."

They didn't like it. It was a dead star, with a pocket of rare transuranic element on it, such as a burned-out sun sometimes creates during the long aeons of its dying.

When they had landed and were sweating in their special heavy-grav suits to cut the ore, there was a grumble from Janssen, ordinarily the lightest-hearted of the Mercs.

"I don't much like this place."

Chane agreed. To a spaceman, the great suns were

23

the blazing, radiating life of the universe. It was an oppressive thing to stand upon the corpse of a star.

The vast dark cindery plain, rising into low ridges of slag, was somber and sad beneath the starry sky. They cut away with the ato-torches, but even with the mechanical-assist devices built into the heavy-grav suits every move they made was toilsome. Chane was used to heavy gravity, but nothing this heavy. Through the helmet-intercom he could hear Bollard puffing noisily.

"Chane," said Bollard, "this is a pretty clever plan you dreamed up, collecting precious ores to take with us to Mruun."

"I thought it was pretty clever," Chane said.

"Just do me a favor," said Bollard, "and next time don't get clever at the expense of my aching back."

They finally got the ore into the hold and left the dead star. Again they coasted the enormous dark nebula, using the probe of the analyzer on every likely-looking mass of drift within range, but with no result.

They angled away from the cloud and soon made passage through a mighty triplet of blazing suns, two of them yellow and the third a yellowish green. Chane knew them well, for they were a famous starmark on the old Varnan road.

Chane had told Dilullo about a freak star-system beyond this triplet, and they pulled cautiously toward it. It was one of the curious systems found here and there which mothered comets instead of planets. A bewildering shoal of elliptical comets spun about the white star, looking like brilliant moths around a flame.

The ship drove through them. Comets were a large bunch of nothing, except for a possible nucleus of meteoric material, but they could play the devil with instruments. Dilullo took it cautiously, and finally set them down on one of the asteroids, the nearest thing to a planet this sun possessed.

No rock-hoppers had been here, and the first sweep of the analyzer located terbium and tantalum. In a comparatively short time they had what they needed in the hold and Dilullo was feeling his way back out through the comets.

"And now," he told Chane in his cabin later, "Mruun. And it's up to you to find the Singing Suns."

Chane looked at him. "You don't much like this one, do you, John?"

"Let's say," answered Dilullo, "I don't much like the Argo Spur. Its name is a stink and an abomination in the galaxy, and not only just because the Starwolves lair there."

It was on the tip of Chane's tongue to ask why he had come if he felt that way, but he did not ask. He knew why Dilullo had come.

"Well," said Chane, "it may cheer you up to hear that while we'll all be in danger at Mruun, I'll be in a special added danger."

"At the moment, that does sort of cheer me up," said Dilullo.

Chane grinned. "I thought it would."

IV

IN THE STEAMY, suffocating night of Mruun, the big city throbbed with life and sound. Going through its crowded streets with Chane, Dilullo thought that although he had been on many queer worlds, he had never seen anything like this before.

The Mruunians themselves might have been human once. . . . Earthmen had discovered when they first got the star-drive that they had had predecessors, a forgotten star-traveling human race that in the remote past had seeded much of the galaxy with humanity. But time and evolutionary pressures had changed the original stock in many ways. The natives of Mruun were now gray-skinned, Humpty-Dumpty types with big pot bellies, small short legs and narrow faces. They were extremely polite as they waddled through the streets, and their faces had a calm malice in them; Dilullo did not like them at all.

But the gray natives were only a part of the incredibly motley crowd that thronged under the lurid orange lights of these bazaar streets. Beaked and feathered men strode along, regarding everything with unwinking yellow eyes. Bulky, white-skinned creatures with elephantine legs smiled blandly as they went along. There were some who wore cloaks and hoods as though they did not want to show their bodies at all. Then over the buzz and hum of the street came an outburst of yelping laughter as a bunch of furry near-men who looked like big bear-dogs walking erect swayed drunkenly into a tavern.

"They're from Paragara," Chane said. "Not a bad lot but not very good with spaceships."

"They look to me," said Dilullo, "like a lot of country boys who have come to the wicked city and are about to be taken for all they have."

Chane nodded. Dilullo noticed that as Chane went along, carrying their sack of ore samples easily with one hand, his eyes kept shifting here and there over the throng, his dark face wary and alert.

He remembered what Chane had said to him when they had left the Merc ship at the spaceport.

"I'm known as a Starwolf on Mruun, John. Not only

by old Klloya-Klloy, to whom I've sold a lot of loot, but by others here, including off-worlders. That's why I don't want anyone but you with me, or the Mercs are likely to find out all about me."

It had taken all Dilullo's authority to keep the others confined to the ship, but he had managed it by his assertion that they were needed to guard the ship and its equipment on this thieves' market world. Looking at the faces of this crowd, faces human and nonhuman but nearly all steeped in the wickedness of the Spur worlds, Dilullo felt that his assertion had not been far wrong.

Drinking places from which loud voices spoke, barked, or howled, cook-shops from which drifted odors that were partly delectable and partly nauseous, brothels where God knew what went on . . . the place made any of the Star Street quarters of the main galaxy look like a kindergarten. He was glad when they got into a less crowded section of large shops. They were mostly shut at this hour, but their barred windows displayed silks and jewels and outlandish sculptures, loot of many raided worlds sold here quite openly.

Chane casually turned down a narrow and dark side way. He glanced around as they went, but there was no one in sight. He darted suddenly off the dark street into a still darker area behind the buildings that housed the shops.

Dilullo, following him, said, "And what the devil are we going to do here?"

"Keep your voice down, John," whispered Chane. "I am going to engage in a bit of burglary and you are going to wait for me, that's what we're going to do."

"Burglary? That's nice," said Dilullo. "Do you mind telling me what you're going to steal?"

"You promised to let me run this operation," Chane said. "All will be explained to you. But to ease your conscience, stealing is considered the highest form of art on Mruun, and nearly everything in all these shops is stolen property."

He hunkered down and in the darkness Dilullo could see that he was fishing something out of the sack of samples. It was a small cylindrical object which Chane fastened to his coverall by a clip. He touched it and it began a faint, almost inaudible buzzing.

"An alarm-damper," said Chane. "Every one of these places is guarded in ways you can't imagine, but I think this will take me through the first beams without setting them off."

"So this is what you were so busy making on our way here in the ship?"

"This and a couple of other things," Chane said. "But there's one instrument I can't possibly make, and that's what I have to steal here. You see, this shop specializes in highly sophisticated instruments of crime."

With that he was gone, moving like a shadow through the darkness to the back of the low building. Dilullo examined his stunner, and then sat down on the edge of the sample sack to avoid sitting on the damp ground.

The air was oppressive, like a steam bath. There were few sounds here except the murmur of the distant uproar in the main streets. Dilullo mopped his face and wondered why in the world he should be sitting in this damp hellhole when he could have been taking his ease in Brindisi.

Well, he knew the answer to that one and there was

no use thinking about it, and he had better just sit and hope Chane didn't set off something that would get them both killed.

After a few minutes he heard a low sound from the dark building, like the sound of a voice abruptly cut off. Dilullo jumped erect and stood with his stunner in his hand.

Nothing happened. He stood there for what seemed quite a long time, and then a shadow came toward him. He could not identify the figure in the dark and he did not want to raise his voice in a challenge, so he just gambled that it was Chane coming back.

It was. Chane held in his hand a cubical thing that looked like some kind of instrument. He squatted down with it, and rummaged in the sample sack until he found what he wanted and dragged it out. It was a sheet of palladium, and Dilullo remembered how, on the way to Mruun, Chane had hammered on a sample of the metal to make that sheet.

"If I'm not interrupting you . . ." Dilullo said politely.

"No interruption at all," said Chane. "What is it?"

As he spoke he was bending the sheet of palladium and wrapping it all around the cubical thing he had brought out of the dark shop.

"Were there guards in there?" Dilullo asked.

"There were," said Chane. "Two of them. And to answer your next question, I didn't kill them. I was a good little Earthman like you said, and only stunned them."

"Now what?" said Dilullo.

Chane, working away in the dark, did not look up as he answered, "We want to know where the Singing Suns are. All right. There's only one merchant on Mruun big enough to buy them from the Starwolves, and if he didn't, he'll know who did. That's Klloya-Klloy, and he'll need a little inducing. That's what this instrument is for. You could call it an inducer."

He finished wrapping the palladium sheet completely around the cubical box, and then put the thing down into the sack of ore samples and stood up.

"You see," said Chane, "we'll be scanned from the moment we go into Klloya-Klloy's place. We'd never get past the first gate with this thing. But with the palladium wrapped around it, the scanner-rays will see it as just another ore sample."

Dilullo shook his head. "Do you know, Chane, I'm kind of glad I came with you on this. It's educational. That's what it is, real educational."

He expected Chane to lead him to one of the big shops in the bazaar, but instead Chane went through more dark side streets into an area of large villas. One of these had a high wall around its extensive grounds, and a gate in the wall with two enormous yellow men standing guard.

Chane spoke to them in galacto, the lingua franca of the galaxy. "We've something to sell. These are samples."

"Weapons," said one of the guards, extending his hand.

Chane handed over his stunner, and Dilullo followed his example, though he did not like doing it. He was sure from what Chane had said that from somewhere in the gatehouse beside them they and their sack were being thoroughly examined by scanning rays.

A voice spoke a word from inside the guardhouse, and the yellow guards stood aside to let them enter.

"Fallorians," said Chane as they walked toward the villa. "Real tough men. Klloya-Klloy has a lot of them."

"You know," said Dilullo, "I'm beginning to wonder where my brains were when I came along with you."

The villa was a big mansion, and there was the loom of even bigger warehouses in the grounds behind it. They went into a lobby that was garishly decorated with fabulous-looking art pieces from many worlds, all in utterly conflicting styles. A couple more of the huge yellow men lounged here, and a young Mruunian sat behind a desk.

He said, "Ore samples, eh? I hope you have enough of the stuff to make it worth our while to bother."

Chane said, "I'll talk that over with Klloya-Klloy."

The Mruunian tittered maliciously. "Rock-hoppers wanting to deal personally with the master. What will we have next?"

Chane smiled and reached across the desk and grabbed the Mruunian up out of his chair. "Tell Klloya-Klloy that Morgan Chane the Starwolf wants to see him, or I'll drive my fist right through you, little pudding."

"Starwolf?" The Mruunian looked shaken. "Now I remember you. But—"

A voice came from the communic on the desk. "I heard that. Let him in."

A door opened at the far end of the lobby. Chane picked up his sack and Dilullo followed him into a surprisingly small office. The door closed silently behind them.

In one of the dish-shaped things that passed for chairs on this world, an amazingly fat Mruunian sat, his whole obesity shaking with his laughter. But his small eyes remained cold.

"Morgan Chane," he said. "Well, well, I heard that they ran you out of the Starwolves."

"They did," said Chane. "And I took to prospecting, with some friends. And I found something big."

"It would have to be big," said Klloya-Klloy. "You know me well enough from the old days. . . . I never touch anything small."

"Wait till you see this," said Chane.

He took out of the sack the square, palladium-wrapped object. He set it down on the desk before Klloya-Klloy. With his two hands he tore the palladium sheathing suddenly away, revealing a cubical instrument from which there extended a cord whose bifurcated tips ended in flat black metal disks.

The instant he saw the instrument, Klloya-Klloy reacted violently. His chubby arm darted toward a row of buttons on the desk.

Chane was too fast for him. With one hand he covered the Mruunian's mouth, and his other arm encircled the obese body and pulled it, chair and all, away from the desk.

Dilullo, utterly astonished, stood goggling. Chane hissed to him, urgently.

"Quick, get the deherer disks over his head. One on each side. *Quick!*"

V

DILULLO grabbed the cord and applied the disks to each side of the struggling Mruunian's head. The disks were connected by a spring that held them in place. Then, at Chane's direction, Dilullo snicked on the two switches in the side of the small cubical instrument.

At once Klloya-Klloy stopped struggling. He sat stony still in the dish-like chair and his narrow eyes became glazed and expressionless.

Chane let go of him and stepped back a little. Dilullo said, "I've heard of these things, though I never saw one. It's a shorter, isn't it?"

Chane nodded. "It is. Shortcuts the will completely and makes truthful responses mandatory."

"And the things are illegal on every world," said Dilullo.

Chane smiled. "Nothing is illegal on Mruun. Now stand by."

He turned and spoke to Klloya-Klloy. "Did the Varnans bring the Singing Suns to Mruun to sell?"

Klloya-Klloy answered tonelessly, staring blank-eyed straight ahead. "Yes."

"Did you buy them?"

"I did not buy them. The sum was too great. I acted as agent."

"To whom did you sell them?"

"Eron of Rith, six. Iqbard of Thiel, four. Klith . . ." He named off several names and the number of Suns purchased until they were all accounted for, ending up with, ". . . and the Qajars, ten."

"The Qajars?" Chane frowned. "I never heard of them. Who are they? What is their world?"

"A planet in the dark cluster DB-444 beyond the Spur."

Chane's frown deepened. "There's no inhabited world in that cluster."

Klloya-Klloy remained silent. No direct question had been put to him, so he made no answer.

"Where is the cluster?" asked Dilullo. He was asking Chane, but Klloya-Klloy heard the question.

"Celestial latitude and longitude are . . ."

He began to reel off figures and Dilullo noted them down. But Chane still scowled.

"There are no people out there rich enough to buy ten of the Singing Suns," he muttered.

"Look," said Dilullo. "We've stuck our heads into the lion's jaws to get this information . . . though I'll admit this character looks more like a turnip than a lion. Hadn't we better get out of here?"

Chane nodded. "I think you're right."

"How do we do it?"

Chane shrugged. "We just walk out. The shorter will keep him sitting here until someone comes in and takes it off his head."

They walked out. They went through the lobby, loftily ignoring the young Mruunian at the desk, and out of the big building. At the gatehouse, the yellow Fallorian guards gave them back their stunners.

They went down the dark street twenty paces, and then a screeching, hell-roaring siren let go behind them in the villa grounds and Chane said, "*Run!*"

Dilullo could not run with Chane's Starwolf speed but he stretched his legs and did his best. Chane reached an arm to help him along and Dilullo struck it angrily aside, and Chane laughed and said, "Your pride is going to get you killed one of these times, John."

When they got into the crowded bazaar streets, Dilullo's hopes picked up. But then he looked back and saw a low car with the big yellow Fallorian guardsmen in it turn into the street.

The motley mob was too dense for the car to get through. The Fallorians piled out of it and came after them, plowing massively through the throng.

Dilullo, glancing back, did not watch where he was going and collided with a large furry body. The bunch of bear-dog men whom Chane had called Paragarans had just come out of a drinking place. They were now

34

very drunk indeed and the one Dilullo had careered into went off his feet, and Dilullo with him.

Chane reached down and yanked Dilullo erect. The bear-dog men milled around, staring at them in a fuddled way.

"We've had it," said Dilullo.

The Fallorians had overtaken them and were roughly pushing aside the bear-dog men to get at them.

It proved to be the wrong thing to do. The bear-dog men were drunk enough to fight anyone who pushed them around. With barking howls they threw themselves at the yellow guards.

The Paragarans were almost as big as the Fallorians and they were ferocious fighters. They went in with their jaws seeking for holds and their arms whirling like furry maces. Chane jumped in with them, using all his Starwolf strength against the Fallorians and not caring who saw him.

The thing became a swirling brawl. Dilullo stood apart from it, with his stunner in his hand. There was no chance to use the weapon, the combatants were so closely mixed. Chane seemed to be enjoying himself hugely. He used his fists, his elbows, his feet, his knees, and the butting surface of his head, all with equal agility. It seemed to Dilullo that only a few moments went by before the thing suddenly quieted and the Fallorians were lying insensible or twisted up and groaning.

The dog-like Paragarans slapped Chane on the back with immense, drunken joviality. Then one of them, looking owlishly wise, spoke to the others in a husky, barking voice. They all started away from there, weaving a bit and sort of leaning against the crowd. The crowd made way for them very rapidly.

Chane, mopping his brow, grinned after them. "They think they had all better go back to Paragara," he said. "I know a little bit of their language."

"I think they're right," said Dilullo sourly. "And maybe we'd just better emulate their example and get back to our own ship. I'd like to get the devil out of here—if we still can. Your friend Klloya-Klloy may have alerted the spaceport security officers."

"That's the beauty of a world like Mruun," said Chane. "No security officers. No law. If you've got anything valuable you hire guards to look after it for you. It's up to you, completely."

"A nice kind of world," said Dilullo. "For a Starwolf, that is. Wait a minute. . . ."

He had spotted one of the furry Paragarans, lying senseless in the street not far from the yellow guards. He raised his voice and yelled after the Paragarans who were receding into the darkness.

"Come back here!" he yelled in galacto. "You've left one behind."

"They don't hear you," said Chane. "Too drunk."

"What will happen to this one?" asked Dilullo, frowning down at what ridiculously resembled a gigantic teddy bear dropped by a passing child, only the child would have to be ten feet high.

"I expect the Fallorians will cut his throat if they catch him," said Chane, quite unconcerned.

Dilullo rapped out an oath he rarely used. "No. We'll take him with us. Pick him up."

Chane stared. "Are you out of your mind? Why should we bother with him?"

Dilullo got a wintry edge to his voice. "Every now and then, Chane, I have to remind myself that you're not altogether human. Well, I am. And anyone who fights on my side, I don't leave behind to get killed. Not even a damned Starwolf."

Chane laughed suddenly. "You've got me there, John. I remember back on Arkuu when that damned fanatic Helmer had us pinned on the mountainside, you came chasing back up to see if I was dead or living."

He picked up the unconscious Paragaran and slid him across his shoulders. He winced as he did so.

"He's big and heavy," Dilullo said. "Let me give you a hand."

"It's not the weight, it's the stench of him," said Chane. "This critter smells like a one-man tavern."

He started forward down the street, and on Mruun, where everybody minds his own business, nobody even looked at them. They reached the spaceport road and went along it under the light of the Spur stars.

Dilullo kept looking back but there was no more pursuit as yet. He began to think that with luck they might make it.

Chane, as he stumped along with his furry burden in the steamy dark, uttered a low laugh.

"Fun and games," he said. "Isn't this better than sitting on your backside in Brindisi?"

Dilullo made a sound indicative of disgust. Chane continued, "You know, John, I've often thought of Arkuu . . . and that girl Vreya. I'd like to go back and see her one of these days."

"Leave her alone," said Dilullo. "She's far too good for the likes of you."

The spaceport lights came up and Dilullo kept his hand on the hilt of his stunner, but nothing at all happened.

They went into the ship and Bollard greeted Dilullo with a sweet smile on his moon-fat face.

"Did you have fun?" he asked. "While we were all sitting here with our thumbs up our noses?"

"We had fun," said Dilullo. "There'll be more of the same and enough for all if we don't get off Mruun as fast as we can."

Bollard shouted an order and the Mercs scattered to their posts. Then Chane came in behind Dilullo and dumped his unconscious burden on the deck. Bollard stared at it.

"Who the hell is that?"

"A Paragaran," said Chane. "We sort of got mixed up with him and John felt we couldn't leave him behind."

The hooter sounded as the lock doors slammed shut. They got into the chairs and the little ship went skyward, fast. By the time acceleration eased off and they got out of the recoil chairs, they found that the Paragaran had apparently been revived by the shock of takeoff. He stood up, looking puzzledly around him and swaying gently with an unsteadiness that had nothing to do with takeoff. His gaze lit on Chane and his hairy face split in a pleased grin.

"A damned good fight," he said in galacto in a roaring, husky bellow. He clamped Chane on the back with his great paw. "And you're a good fighter. You brought me out of there?"

Chane shook his head. "Not a bit of it. I'd have left you lying there." He pointed to Dilullo. "But my friend John here is the loyal comrade type. He brought you to save your neck."

The big Paragaran turned and stared at Dilullo with red-rimmed, glazed eyes, and then stepped unsteadily toward him.

"I'm Gwaath," he bellowed. "And I'll tell you this:

anybody does Gwaath a favor like that and he's got a friend for life!"

His furry arm went around Dilullo's neck in a crushing embrace. He looked into Dilullo's face with drunken, doggy affection, and uttered a mighty belch.

Dilullo reeled.

VI

THE SHIP, in overdrive, went farther and farther into the vast wilderness of Argo Spur. It went over great drifts of dust-choked suns whose haggard witch-fires extended for many parsecs. It passed dark shoals where dead stars had long ago collided and filled space with wheeling debris. It skirted a huge tornado-like whirl of dead and living stars that spun ever faster in a mad maelstrom that had a core of neutron stars.

The old Starwolf road, thought Chane, and he knew every star and swarm and dark nebula along the way. And far ahead, on the simulacrum in the bridge, the sun of Varna was a tawny eye watching him, and he looked at it and dreamed.

Presently, over the creaking thrum of the faulty overdrive, Dilullo spoke from behind him.

"I've got half a mind to give up the whole thing and go back to Earth."

"Losing your nerve?" said Chane.

"I've told you before, don't try to needle people. You're no good at it. I've got more nerve than you when the chips are down."

Chane thought about that and then said seriously, "I believe you're right. I can do anything as long as it's fun doing it, but you've got some kind of repression and drive. . . ."

"Call it the Puritan conscience," said Dilullo. "And I don't need any amateur psychoanalysis, either. How much chance do we have of getting the six Suns that Eron of Rith has?"

Chane shrugged. "I've never been to Rith but I've heard about it from Varnans who were there. Eron is a tough character. He'd have to be, to live on that planet. . . . It's nothing but storm all the time, they say."

"Nice," said Dilullo. He was about to add something sour, but Gwaath came lumbering into the bridge.

"Oh, for God's sake," muttered Dilullo in English.

"He loves you," said Chane. "You saved his life, remember? That's why he keeps following you around all the time."

Gwaath's large form seemed to crowd the whole bridge. He patted Dilullo on the shoulder in breezy camaraderie, almost knocking him to the deck.

"How's it going?" the Paragaran asked, in English. "How's everything, old boy?"

Dilullo stared at him. "So you've been picking up things?"

Gwaath nodded, then switched to galacto to explain. "The men down in the crewroom have taught me a little of your language. Listen to this. . . ." And in English he started off a stream of expressions that made Chane grin and brought from Dilullo a hasty demand to stop.

"They *would* teach you things like that," said Dilullo.

"Why, man, children know stronger language than that on Paragara," said Gwaath. "On Paragara—"

Dilullo interrupted. "Look," he said desperately. "Are you sure you don't want us to set you down on some world here in the Spur? Some world where you could get a message to your ship? Then your friends could pick you up."

"I told you before, they're no friends of mine anymore," Gwaath rumbled. "They deserted me there on Mruun, left me to be killed." He added, with an air of ultimate indictment, "They were *drunk*."

Chane did not laugh. The Paragarans might look like big fubsy bear-dogs, but their renown as fighters had gone all through the Spur and they were quick to take offense.

"No," Gwaath was saying, "I'll stick with you till we hit some world where I can get to Paragara on my own. Where do you touch first?"

"Rith," said Dilullo.

"Hell of a place," said Gwaath. "If it isn't raining it's hailing or lightning and it usually does all three together."

"You've been there?" asked Dilullo.

"Two—three times," said Gwaath. "The people of Rith buy some herbs that are raised only on Paragara. When the herbs are dried and then burned, they do very strange things to the mind."

"Who is Eron of Rith?" asked Dilullo.

Gwaath stared. "The ruler. They don't go for all that stuff about democratic government on Rith. One planet, one boss. Eron is it."

Dilullo looked inquiringly at Chane. Chane knew what he meant, and nodded.

"I'll tell you what, Gwaath," said Dilullo. "We're going to Rith on a kind of risky mission. And I think you ought to know what it is before you go along with us."

He told Gwaath about the Singing Suns. The Paragaran made a sound of admiration.

"And the Starwolves got them? Just what I'd expect.

41

Ah, those Varnans are bastards but there's no more bold and clever thieves in the universe. Even on Paragara we're just as glad the Starwolves let us alone."

"From what Klloya-Klloy told us, Eron of Rith has six of the Suns," said Dilullo. "We want them all, and his six come first."

"How are you going to get them?"

"Take them," said Dilullo. "This Eron knew bloody well they were stolen property when he bought them. If we can return them to their rightful owners at Achernar, there's a huge reward waiting for us."

Gwaath's small bright eyes began to gleam in his furry face. "It sounds like fun," he said. "The Rith are a tough lot. Not as tough as the Starwolves or the Paragarans, but tough enough. Even so, it might be done."

"You know Rith, we don't," said Dilullo. "If you want to join in on this there's a share of the reward for you at the end." He added, "Of course, the Mercs have to vote you in first."

The Paragaran did not take long to decide. He shrugged massive shoulders and grinned a grin that showed formidable teeth.

"I might as well," he said. "My ship's gone without me. We were going to become fighters for a kinglet on a Spur world whose subjects are rebellious. Probably there's no more risk looking for the Suns."

"All right," said Dilullo. "I was wondering what excuse for landing we'd make when we set down on Rith. But this takes care of it. . . . we're setting down to put ashore a Paragaran crewman we picked up from a world where he was beached."

"Fine," said Gwaath. "What's your plan for getting the Suns away from Eron, once we're on Rith?"

"Yes, John, what is your plan?" asked Chane, straight-faced. "I've been waiting to hear it."

Dilullo gave him a slightly nasty look. "You'll hear it when I'm ready to tell you. Come along with me, Gwaath. I want to ask some questions about the set-up of Eron's city."

Gwaath cleared his throat. "Well, you see, I was pretty drunk each time I visited the place and I might not remember things so clearly if I was cold sober. I mean—"

Dilullo interrupted. "Two drinks, that's all." He added, surveying the massive figure, "I'll make them large ones, considering your size."

When the ship finally came out of overdrive near Rith, Chane was piloting. The blue-shining sun of this system was a small one, and Rith itself was not a very large world. They could not see much of it because the surface was blanketed under heavy clouds.

Janssen gave Dilullo the readings which gave the location of the radio beacon at Eron City starport.

"At least, I *think* it's the location," said Janssen unhappily. "There's the devil and all of a thunderstorm covering that whole region, and most of what I got was in little bits and pieces."

He went back into the radar room. Dilullo studied the readings. Then, instead of handing them to Chane, he spoke into the intercom.

"Sekkinen, you come up to the bridge for pilot duty."

Chane looked around at him. "I'm perfectly capable of taking her in."

Dilullo nodded. "I know you are. But it's going to be tricky in that storm and I'd just as lief not have a

Starwolf type of pilot who thinks hell, let's take a chance, and slams us right into the middle of the city."

"John, you remember things too well. You ought to learn to take it as it comes."

But he made no other complaint, and yielded the pilot chair to Sekkinen when he came.

Sekkinen was a born complainer. He complained now about the fact that it was not his turn at duty, about the injustice of asking a man to home in on fragmentary radar readings, and about the fact that he hadn't been allowed to finish his dinner.

He went on and on, but while he complained his hands were moving swiftly and surely and the little ship went down into the cloud-masses and the storm.

They were descending toward the night side of the planet, but the incessant sheets of lightning made it frequently brighter than day. The winds, as registered on the board, were terrific; they would have known that anyway from the buffeting. The flaring atmospherics broke and distorted the sensor rays of the ship's instruments so that it lurched about half blind. Sekkinen kept complaining and all the time his hands kept moving skillfully. Presently the lightning-flares showed a small starport rushing up toward them, and when they bumped down onto it Dilullo sighed with relief.

"Listen to that," said Chane, when the power had been turned off.

The ship was being smashed at by rain that fell in great solid chunks rather than as drops. The drumming roar of it was deafening.

"We can't go out into that; it'd knock our heads off," said Dilullo. "We'll wait."

They waited. The drumming downpour continued. It was well over an hour before it suddenly stopped.

"All right," said Dilullo. "Just Bollard and Gwaath and me, for now. Crack the lock."

They went out into chill, damp darkness. Dilullo saw the lights of what he took to be starport administration and started toward them. The other two followed, Gwaath's big feet splashing in the puddles.

Suddenly they were washed by a fierce glare of spotlights from ahead of them. At the same moment a hard voice spoke to them in galacto from an amplifier.

"There are four heavy lasers trained on your ship," it said metallically. "Every man aboard is to come out, without weapons, and walk in this direction."

"What is this?" demanded Dilullo loudly. "We're an Earth prospecting craft, and we only set down here to land a stranded Paragaran. . . ."

"Just keep walking, my innocent Earthman," said the harsh voice. "Eron wants to see you. He knows exactly why you have come to Rith."

VII

It is not often, Dilullo thought, *that you see a thoroughly happy man. It does your heart good to see one.*

Eron of Rith was a happy man. He strutted back and forth, a small man with a tough, faintly red face and bristling black hair, looking for all the world like a falcon turned human. He laughed and slapped his sides and laughed again, looking toward the table where Dilullo and Chane and Gwaath were sitting.

"It's so damned *funny*," he said in galacto. "You just don't realize yet how funny it is."

Dulillo drank a little, not much, of the fiery Rith

liquor they had been served. He said mildly, "Let us in on the joke. What makes it so funny?"

Eron shook his head and laughed and kept striding back and forth. He was small, but he threw a big shadow across the stone floor of the great barny banqueting hall.

Men stood around it here and there at a respectful distance, well out of hearing. Red-skinned men of Rith, powerful runts with lasers and stunners. Their eyes never left the three men at the table.

The room was cold and utterly unwelcoming. On its walls in a sort of palimpsest over blurred old paintings of gracious blue people in gardens were daubed crude, violent figures of small red men carrying weapons in war. Once there had been a gentler civilization here, Dilullo knew, and then the fierce outlanders or outworlders had come. It was an old story; one met it all over the galaxy.

Eight girls danced, almost naked, at the far end of the long shadowy hall. None of them were of the red Rith people; they were of various colors, tall, and they danced with a lazy, sinuous grace to the twanging of hidden musicians. Nobody watched them. They were a decoration, not a performance.

Dilullo waited, saying nothing more. Eron was so full of himself and his triumph that he would sooner or later start talking. In the meantime, the Mercs were all under guard in an upper wing of this sprawling old palace, and only he and Chane and Gwaath had been brought here.

Gwaath was pretty happy himself. Lots of the fiery Rith liquor had been set before them and the Paragaran had quaffed it in truly heroic quantities. He sat in a bit of a daze, his furry face leering foolishly at Eron, like a schoolgirl admiring a hero. There was something so ridiculous about his expression that Dilullo felt like laughing.

There was nothing about Chane that made him feel like laughing. Chane had got pretty drunk, and this was a surprise. Dilullo had seen him drink a good bit at times, but it had always seemed only to deepen the mocking irony in his dark face. But Chane looked black as a thundercloud now, and the exquisitely measured deliberation of his movements told Dilullo how drunk he was.

Homesick, thought Dilullo. *He's got back out here to the Spur, and Varna is not too far away as galactic distances go; but he can never go back there and it's eating on him.*

"Didn't you ever dream," said Eron, "that Klloya-Klloy might send messages to all of us who bought the Singing Suns, to warn us that Mercs were out to get them?"

Dilullo shrugged. "We thought of the possibility. We supposed that Klloya-Klloy would not want to advertise the fact that we'd come right into his headquarters and twisted his nose. It wouldn't be good publicity for a famous receiver of stolen goods."

"You were wrong," said Eron. "Klloya-Klloy doesn't care whether it's good or bad publicity. He was so angry he just wanted you caught and punished."

Dilullo nodded. "It figures. But I'm leader of the mission. Why bring Gwaath and Chane up here for your gloating?"

Eron said, "As to the Paragaran, I'm just curious as to what he's doing with you. You might say he's just for laughs."

Gwaath responded to this by a tipsy smile that split his formidable face open and showed his gleaming teeth. It was a sort of I-love-you-too smile. Then he put his head down on the table and snored.

"As for the man Chane," Eron continued after a moment, "Klloya-Klloy mentioned him. Morgan Chane, the Starwolf. How can an Earthman be a Starwolf?"

Chane drained his goblet and set it down. He said, "But I'm not a Starwolf."

He got up and stepped around the table toward Eron. The little red men around the hall raised their weapons a trifle. The naked girls continued to dance to the twanging strings. On the walls the dim, gentle-faced blue people smiled from behind the striding little crimson warriors painted over them.

Chane's face assumed a sweet smile, and Dilullo thought, *For God's sake, not that. I've seen that smile before and it means trouble.*

"You see," said Chane to Eron, "I'm only half Starwolf. I was born on Varna and I grew up with the Varnans and raided with them, but I was never anything more than half a Varnan, I realize now."

And then of a sudden Chane's voice rasped like a sword coming out of its scabbard. "But half a Starwolf is enough to merit respect from the little lesser breeds like the men of Rith!"

Rage flared up in Eron's small eyes. He half raised his hand to summon the men with weapons who were ranged around the walls of the big stone room.

He did not complete the motion. He looked at Chane with something like admiration in his face.

"You're a Starwolf, all right," he said. "Only one of those devils would say a thing like that, here where I could crook my finger and have you killed."

Chane shrugged. "I'll tell you how the Varnans see it, and how they taught me. A man can get killed any time, and in any case he can't live forever, so there's no use worrying about it."

"Why aren't you with the Varnans?" demanded Eron. "What are you doing with these Mercs?"

"A disagreement," Chane said carelessly. "I killed a comrade who tried to kill me, and I had no clan to back me up. So I got out."

"In other words," said Eron, "you ran."

"Of course I ran. Starwolves are realists. They don't want to be killed any more than anyone else does. The point is that they just don't worry so damned much about it."

Eron laughed suddenly and clapped him on the back. "Have another drink," he said. "I've got a funny story to tell you men. It's so funny you'll just about die laughing."

And here it comes, thought Dilullo, *the little surprise that has kept him so happy.*

"You came here," said Eron, "to snatch away the six Singing Suns that I bought from Klloya-Klloy."

"There doesn't seem to be any point in denying it," Dilullo said sourly.

"That's where the joke comes in," said Eron. "I do not have the Singing Suns."

Dilullo stared at him. "But you just admitted that you bought them from Klloya-Klloy."

"I did," said Eron. He had to stop and laugh again before he went on. "But I don't have them. You see, the joke is not only on you, but on Klloya-Klloy too. And to think he took the trouble to send me a warning . . ."

He was off into mirth again. Dilullo had a fair bit of patience but it was beginning to wear thin.

"If you don't mind," he said, "I'd like to hear the

point of this wonderful joke and then I can laugh along with you."

"The point," said Eron, "is that all the Singing Suns were bought by one purchaser. The Qajars. They used the rest of us as purchasing agents. If they'd bid for all the Suns, Klloya-Klloy's price would have been like the ransom for a star. So they only bid for some of them and had the rest of us—all that list of buyers the old merchant gave you—buy the other Suns in piece lots. We delivered them and now the Qajars have all the Singing Suns."

Chane, despite his dark and bitter mood, laughed aloud. "A neat trick. They foxed the old spider of Mruun very nicely."

"Neat is the word for it," Eron agreed cheerfully. "So you can understand why, when Klloya-Klloy rushed me a warning and you Mercs came cleverly sneaking to Rith with all sorts of plans to take my six Suns, I thought it was really funny."

"It's so funny I'm speechless," Dilullo said. "So the Qajars have all the Suns? Who the hell are the Qajars, anyway?"

"People," said Eron. "Very odd people. They're aesthetes, probably the greatest lovers of beautiful things in the galaxy. They are also extremely clever with weapons. And they have no bowels of mercy in them. You think we Rith are tough and ruthless—"

"I don't," said Chane.

Eron shot him an irritated look, but then went on. "Besides the Qajars, we're tender as maidens. I just can't figure them out. They have the most beautiful and valuable objects ever heard of and they love them the way a man loves his newest slave-girl. I could understand their wanting to defend them. But their weapons are not built just for efficiency. They're deliberately designed to torture as well as kill, and the Qajars delight in using them."

"They sound like charming people. And they have all the Singing Suns?"

"They have all the Singing Suns."

"Where is their world?"

Eron smiled. "I've been there often. Last time I took the six Singing Suns. And you know what . . . ?" He had to stop to laugh again. "I landed on their world and I took tridim pictures of all their treasures and they never even knew it. They'd have killed me if they had, they're so secretive."

Chane looked at him. "The man asked you a question. Where is their world?"

"Ah," said Eron, "of course you want to know that. I thought you would. And maybe I'll tell you. Maybe. You see, the Qajars have kept themselves and their treasures utterly hidden. I'm one of the very few people who could tell you about them."

"I seem to smell some kind of deal coming up," Dilullo said sourly. "All right, get to it."

"We have heard," said Eron, "that the government of Achernar is offering a two million credit reward for the return of the Singing Suns. That reward is what you Mercs are after, isn't it?"

"I don't see any point in denying that, either," said Dilullo.

"You haven't got a prayer of getting to the Qajars and the Suns on your own," said Eron. "You don't know where their world is, and even if you knew, your ship would never reach it. They've got defenses like you never heard of."

Dilullo eyed him and said, "Go on."

"But," said Eron, his small eyes very bright, "I could direct you straight to them. I could lend you a small Rith scout that would fool them into letting you land. My tridims would show you just where the Suns are. All this I would do . . . for half of those two million credits."

He added, "Of course, a Rith scout is small. Only three or four of you could go in it. The rest would be my guests here . . . and a guarantee that you'd return."

"In other words," said Dilullo, "having foxed Klloya-Klloy as an agent for the Qajars, you are now willing to betray your employers to us."

Eron grinned. "That's it."

"At least," Dilullo said, "you do put a high price on your loyalty." Then he asked, "Will you tell me . . . is there a single honest man in Argo Spur?"

Eron stared. He turned to Chane and said, "Did you hear that, Starwolf? He's looking for an honest man in the Spur!"

And both Chane and Eron roared with laughter at the idea.

VIII

A SMALL cluster of dead, dark stars, with only a few nearly extinct suns showing a dull red light. . . . It was a lonely and desolate spectacle as the tridim projector showed it in the shadowy hall.

"I know that cluster," said Chane. "It's clear outside the Spur, in a nadir-westward direction."

"Right," said Eron.

"But there's no inhabited world in there."

"Wrong, this time. The Qajars live there, on the

planet of one of those dying suns, deep in the cluster. They call it Chlann."

Chane looked incredulous. "Nobody, not even the Varnans, has ever heard of it."

Eron smiled. "That's because the Qajars want it that way. They're one of the richest peoples in the galaxy and because of that they remain carefully hidden."

"Rich? What is there in that mess of dead suns and frozen worlds that would make them rich?" demanded Dilullo.

"There's radite," said Eron. "The rarest transuranic element of all. There are tremendous deposits of radite on their world, which is why they came there originally. You know the price that stuff brings."

Dilullo still looked skeptical. "How the devil could they sell it and still keep their existence secret?"

"Simple," said Eron. "They use a few selected people in the Spur as their agents. I have been one of them. We go into the cluster and pick up the radite, which is our pay for bringing them back the things they want. And the things they want are always costly, and beautiful, and difficult to steal."

"I'll be damned," said Dilullo. "They sound worse than that thieves' race on Mruun."

"The Qajars are a lot worse," said Eron. "I'm convinced they're more than a little mad . . . that the emanations of radite have had a genetic effect on their minds. They never leave that hidden world. They stay there and fondle their treasures and invent ever more ingenious and unpleasant weapons with which to guard them, and all the time they acquire more and more of the rarest art-treasures in the galaxy so they'll have more to guard. And if that isn't madness, what is?"

Chane mentally pricked up his ears. "It sounds like a fine place to loot."

Eron nodded. "Exactly why they've kept themselves a secret. But nobody would get their treasures easily. The Qajars are infinitely cruel and very cunning, and they have many defenses. Like the Lethal Worlds."

"The Lethal Worlds?"

Eron pointed to the pictured dark cluster. "The Qajars say they have mined many of the dead planets in that cluster with sufficient charges of radite to explode them like huge bombs. They could destroy any fleet that came against them."

Chane said contemptuously, "It sounds like a bluff to scare people away."

"I wouldn't count on it," said Eron. "I know myself they're absolutely without scruple or mercy. In fact—" He hesitated. "In fact, I had a feeling that after they got all the Singing Suns together the Qajars would start doing away with the agents who procured them, so no one would ever know. I wouldn't go into that cluster again!"

"But you're suggesting we go in," said Dilullo.

Eron grinned. "That's different. If you get hurt I won't feel it."

He made a signal and the tridim picture changed. They seemed now to be hanging above the surface of a nearly-dead planet. Black, arid plains swept away to low, dark mountains, all the landscape illumined dimly by the feeble red rays of the dying sun.

At one point on the plain rose a small city. Its buildings were of glittering metal. They were of no great size, most of them, but the center of the city was a round open area, and around this plaza there rose a ring of soaring metal towers. Over the whole place brooded a glow of blue radiance that seemed quite sourceless.

"That halo gives them light and warmth," said Eron. "They have radite enough to maintain a thousand like it."

Dilullo noted the ships parked on a big starport. "I thought you said these Qajars never left their world."

"They don't," said Eron. "Those are all warships, for defense."

"Are those tall towers their treasure houses?" asked Chane.

"You've got a Starwolf's eye for loot, all right," said Eron. "Yes, they are. I've never been allowed inside them, but my concealed tridim camera, using sensor rays, got pictures of the interiors."

The picture changed to the interior of a big room whose walls were softly-burnished metal. And there were people in this room.

The Qajars. Tall men and women in white robes. They had pure white faces, almost beautiful, and slender hands. Their eyes were dark and wide and calm. But there was a chilling inhumanity about the unnatural placidity of those cold faces.

"I see what you mean about them," muttered Dilullo. "They do look as though progressive genetic change and isolation have twisted them."

Chane was not looking at the Qajars. He was looking at the objects that crowded the room, glittering treasures that drew his gaze like a magnet.

Diamond, pearl, chrysoprase, fire-rubies from the worlds of Betelgeuse, shimmering lightstones from Kharal, the sea green gems that are brought up from under the oceans of Algol Three, gold, silver, electrum, all put together into incredible vases, chairs, panels, and other things he could not even define. They all had overwhelming grace and beauty, but it was not that which made Chane draw in his breath sharply.

"Makes you drool, doesn't it?" said Dilullo. "All that loot."

"And we of Varna never even dreamed of it," muttered Chane.

"I told you the Qajars are masters of cunning," said Eron. "Wait till you see into the other treasure houses."

Mobiles, statuary, tapestries woven of tiny gems, monstrous planetary idols in gleaming precious metals, strange symbols from far stars whose stones flashed like fires, great books of gold whose leaves were silver illuminated with designs in tiny jewels.

And through these rooms, between these stunning objects, walked the men and women of the Qajars, looking with calm gaze to the right and then to the left, inspecting their hoard, drinking in its beauty, savoring it in some strange deep way that other men could not even guess at.

"And that's all they do?" said Chane incredulously. "Gather together all that stuff and then just sit and admire it?"

"I told you they're a little mad," said Eron. He added, "Now look at this."

The final tridim pictures showed first a certain tower, and then the interior of a room in it. It was a big, circular room whose whole interior was black—ceiling, floor, the silken hangings on the walls—black as outer space. And in it, as in a shrine, were the Singing Suns.

Incomplete. There were only twenty-eight of them, not forty. Yet they paled everything seen before. They were varicolored, like stars. Pale green, cold blue, warm gold, dull red . . . gleaming glories that slowly revolved as a group, and also around each other. The whole group of them were only four feet across, and they were contained inside a force-shield above a thick four foot base which contained the power unit for the shield. And the beauty of their shining brought a sigh from Dilullo.

"You can't hear them," said Eron. "Not in this picture. But they say if you can hear them as well as see them, you never want to leave them. Anyway, they've got all forty of them now."

Chane looked and looked at them, and there rose strongly in him the Starwolf lust for loot. "We've got to have them," he muttered. "But how?"

"How about my deal, before I go any further?" demanded Eron.

Chane gestured toward Dilullo. "Talk to him. He's the leader."

Dilullo thought for a while. Then he said to Eron, "The deal is on . . . but only conditionally. There are three steps to this operation: getting there, getting the Singing Suns, and getting out again. What can you provide that's worth a million credits?"

"I can provide you with Step One . . . without which there will be no more steps anyway. On Step Two, I can give you the exact location of the treasure room that holds the Singing Suns, the approaches thereto, and what I know or can guess of the obstacles you'll face." Eron smiled, glancing at Chane. "Once you're down you're on your own. And in the matter of thievery, I bow to the master."

Chane showed the hard edges of his teeth. And Dilullo said, "Let's hear it."

Eron said, "You'll go to Chlann in a Rith scout, using

my charts. You will message that you're coming in with a shipment of *ara* root."

"*Ara* root? What's that?"

Eron nodded toward the snoring Paragaran, who still sprawled with his head on the table.

"They grow it on Paragara. About the only place it will grow. It's some kind of stimulant; I don't know exactly what. Anyway, the Qajars love it. They buy it, but not directly. They never do anything directly. The Paragarans bring it here and we take it to Chlann."

Dilullo remembered what Gwaath had said and nodded. "So we go in a Rith scout, with a message about *ara* root. What then?"

"The Qajars will demand identification before they permit you to land. Visual identification."

"And the minute they see our faces we're dead," said Chane. "Nothing could make us look like Rith. How do we get around that?"

Eron smiled, the small delighted smile of a man charmed by his own cleverness. Again he nodded, indicating Gwaath.

"He does it. He makes the visual identification, and he tells them that he's come on from Rith to inform them that there's been a disaster in the *ara* root fields and there won't be any more of the stuff available for a couple of years . . . except maybe a very small supply for very special customers at, naturally, a very special price. It's the price he wants to discuss with them. The Qajars will be worried enough to let you come in."

"*If*," Dilullo added, "they haven't got sensor equipment that will scan the whole interior of the ship. If they see us that'll blow it, as Chane said."

Eron shrugged. "I can't guarantee that they don't have

such equipment, I don't know. But they've never full-scanned a Rith ship. They're used to us. So I don't see why they'd bother this time."

"Sounds like a fair gamble," said Chane.

Dilullo grunted. "I like a little shorter odds, myself. However . . ."

Chane said, "Let's hear about the treasure room."

Eron told him, partly with the aid of the tridim pictures, partly from memory, partly from shrewd guesswork. When he was through Dilullo looked at Chane and said, "Well?" and Chane nodded slowly. His mouth smiled and there was a kind of light in his eyes. *Wolf-light,* Dilullo thought, and fought down a cold cramping of the guts.

"What about the deal?" asked Eron.

"We'll have to talk it over," said Dilullo.

"All right," said Eron. "But don't take too long. I might change my mind."

"One thing," said Dilullo. "None of my party except me knows that Chane was once a Starwolf. I don't want the others told that."

Eron shrugged. "That's no problem as far as I'm concerned."

Chane said, "Thanks for the solicitude, John."

Dilullo looked at him bleakly. "I'm concerned about the others, not you. If any of them found out the truth they'd refuse to work with you, certainly, and might very possibly kill you. Which would break up the whole job." He nodded toward the snoring Paragaran. "Pick up my friend and bring him along."

"He's got to stop this," said Chane, as he slung the sleeping Gwaath across his shoulders. "It's getting to be a habit."

The other Mercs were in a big barrack-like room two

floors up in another wing of the palace. The single door was guarded by several of the little red men with lasers. A few of the Mercs were sleeping but the others were awake and anxious.

Dilullo told them. Their faces fell, a million credits' worth, and Bollard shook his head emphatically.

"It's too risky, John. Two, three men in a little scout —what chance would you have against all those Qajar weapons?"

"Maybe more chance than you think," said Dilullo. "From what I heard, the Qajars have been immune so long that maybe the last thing they'd expect is three men making a sudden raid on their treasure houses."

"Who would the third man be?" demanded Bollard.

"Chane," said Dilullo.

Bollard got belligerent. "Why Chane, instead of me?"

"Because," said Dilullo, "it was Chane who thought up this whole idea of going after the Singing Suns. If I run into a first-class disaster, I'd sort of like him to share it with me."

"I don't blame you," said Bollard, looking without love at Chane. "All the same, I think you're doing something harebrained."

Chane thought that Dilullo's reason for taking him sounded good enough, but it was not the whole reason, even though there was doubtless much truth in it. The real reason was that this was a Starwolf job and Dilullo needed a Starwolf to do it.

"Look," Dilullo was saying to Bollard, "has it occurred to you that we may not have any choice? Eron is being nice right now because he figures to use us as cat's-paws to take the Suns. If we refuse, I can't very well see Eron waving us a sweet goodbye and wishing us a pleasant trip home."

"You may be right," muttered Bollard. "But if you pull it off and bring the Suns back, can you see Eron allowing us to leave with the Suns to get the reward from Achernar to split with him? If he's got the Suns, why should he split at all?"

"Let's not think of that just now," said Dilullo. "We've got trouble enough right ahead without worrying about what comes after it."

IX

THE LITTLE cluster was a graveyard of stars.

Dead suns, ashen hulks black and cold forever. Almost-dead suns, with little tongues and wreaths of fire on their stony, dark surfaces. Dying suns, red and ominous, most of their planets wrapped in everlasting ice. Such worlds had no interest for Starwolves.

But they had been wrong, Chane thought. The Qajar treasure houses, as he had seen in the tridim pictures, had been enough to make a Starwolf go mad. He thought that if the Qajars had been cunning enough to conceal all that for so long, they would be no mean antagonists.

Dilullo sat in the pilot seat of the fast little scout. Gwaath had claimed loudly that he could handle the ship, but when they gave him the chance his piloting had been hopelessly sloppy.

And Chane had said to Dilullo, "I told you the Paragarans aren't much good in space."

He used English but Gwaath caught the critical tone and snarled, "Use galacto! What did you say about me?"

"I said how lucky we are to have a Paragaran with us to fight, if we get into trouble."

Gwaath glared at Chane with his small red eyes. "You're lying. You can't fool me. You may think I'm stupid—"

"What," Chane interrupted blandly, "would give you that idea?"

Gwaath began to roar, and Dilullo raised his voice to tell them both to shut up.

The little scout went on, and they slept, and took turns at the controls, and ate, and swore at the monotony.

And finally they dropped out of overdrive.

A sun far gone into the dusky redness of age glared at them like a huge bloodshot eye. Around it swung a dark planet that seemed nothing but a barren ball of rock. Chlann. The Qajars. The Singing Suns.

Chane quivered a little, like a hunting animal that sees its prey.

"If what Eron told us about these people is true, we'll be challenged very quickly when we go in to make worldfall," said Dilullo.

He was in the pilot chair. He had set up the audio-visual communic so that its view comprised only a limited area of the interior of the scout. Gwaath was seated in front of the little screen of the communic.

"Are you sure you've got it?" Dilullo asked him.

The Paragaran said emphatically that he was good and damned sure. Dilullo hoped he was. They had drilled him in his speech until he ought to be able to repeat it in his sleep.

"Remember," he said, "you're not to move from that seat. The Qajars must not see either Chane or me."

Chane was giving a final check to the laser controls. The heavy lasers were mounted in the prow of the scout, in deep ports.

"If we can get down into that open circle in one piece," said Chane, "these will open a quick way into the treasure room."

"Tell me again," said Dilullo, "what's going to keep the Qajars from clobbering us the minute we set down. It sounded good when you said it, and I need comforting."

"Two things," said Chane confidently. "One, our lasers trained on their beautiful buildings—they'd rather lose one treasure than lose all. Two, they'll be warned that our power unit is set to blow if the ship is hit. If they destroy us, they destroy their own buildings."

Starwolf reasoning, thought Dilullo; *Starwolf cheek.* He hoped Chane was as good as he thought he was.

"Even so," said Chane, "it'll be touch and go, getting in and getting out with the Suns."

"Keep remembering that," said Dilullo. "And don't get tempted to linger for any more of that dazzling stuff we saw, or you might just linger forever."

They were low over the dark, forbidding planet when a voice spoke sharply from the communic.

Dilullo nodded to Gwaath. Gwaath switched on the visual circuits of the communic. In the small screen appeared the pale face of a Qajar, an elderly man with unnaturally smooth skin and the calm icy eyes of his kind peering from under the cowl of his white robe.

Gwaath spoke in galacto, giving the whole carefully-coached story about blight in the *ara* root and how Eron of Rith had told him he should deal directly with the Qajars and lent him a Rith scout to do it in. He talked about shortage and price and future deliveries, and Chane thought that he was the clumsiest liar he had ever heard in his life. But when he thought about it, the Paragaran wasn't so bad after all. There was a certain disarming, not to say stupid candor about him that made it difficult to doubt him.

The Qajar in the screen seemed to consider for a moment. Then he said, "This matter is without precedent. Put your ship into stationary orbit, while we consider."

Gwaaath said he would do that. He asked, "Can I shut off the visual till you call? It consumes power."

The man in the screen nodded contemptuously. He said, "My name is Vlanalan. You will receive our decision very soon. Until then, any attempt to land will result in instant destruction."

Gwaath switched off the visual. They he turned around and looked at Dilullo with a did-I-do-good? expression.

"That was fine, Gwaath," whispered Dilullo. "Just sit there and wait. . . . I'll put the scout into orbit."

He did that, and they waited. And thought about the next move, the descent toward the starport, the sudden diversion and landing in the open circle among the treasure houses, the thing done so swiftly and unexpectedly as to catch the Qajars quite by surprise. They hoped.

They waited for permission to land. And waited. And as the minutes went by a strange feeling, an uneasiness, came over Chane.

He could not define it. It was not a sixth sense. But Starwolves had their five senses honed to a keenness far beyond normal. And this was the same kind of feeling he had had on Allubane, in the dark jungle before the Nanes jumped him. Something was not quite right.

"I think . . ." he began to whisper.

Dilullo held up a hand sharply to silence him. The

auditory channel of the communic was still open, and Dilullo was signaling that they must not be heard.

More minutes went by, and the little ship went on around the dark planet, and the bloody eye of the dying sun looked down at them.

Like a bolt of lightning, pain ripped through Chane's nervous system. His nerves were afire, electric with agony. He tried to dart to the controls, where Dilullo had suddenly crumpled in the chair with his shaking hands over his face.

He could not make it. He was Morgan Chane, the Earthman who had grown up a Starwolf; he had strength and stamina and speed beyond any man of Earth, beyond any non-Varnan in the galaxy. He was very strong and nothing could stop him.

But now he was a baby, weak, shuddering in agony. He fell on his face and lay with his mouth against the cold deck, his tortured body rippling in long slow rhythms of pain.

He rolled around in a vain attempt to get up, and then sobbed as the agony increased. He saw Gwaath, his red eyes wild, rise and stagger and stumble and then crash into a corner. After that Gwaath got to his knees and swayed back and forth uttering hoarse animal sounds.

Dilullo did not even try to get out of the pilot chair. Dilullo seemed to shrink and shrivel, as though a fiery breath of absolute pain was burning him up.

Chane tried to force himself to act. He was bathed in hot agony, but he had felt agony before. What he had to do was get to his feet, get to the controls, and send the scout out of orbit away from Chlann before they all died or went completely mad, which was going to happen very quickly now, in minutes, perhaps seconds.

Summoning all his fierce Starwolf resolution, he got to his feet. And fell down on his face again.

"Fools," said a cold, remote voice. "Did you think we would let your ship approach without searching it by sensor rays? Especially after we had been warned that Earthmen were trying to take the Suns?"

It was the voice of Vlanalan, speaking from the communic. It lashed them with icy, scornful tones.

"You could have been killed at once, of course. But that is not our way. You must suffer until you realize the blackness of your crime in attempting to steal things of beauty from the Qajars. A ship will come. You will be boarded and brought in to us for further examination. In the meantime, your punishment begins."

As though a switch had been turned, the pain that shredded Chane's nerves was stepped up. Dilullo just sagged farther in the chair. Gwaath started to roar insanely and throw himself against the wall. He did that twice and then fell and lay struggling feebly.

Chane whimpered. He was tough, he had taken pain before, but nothing like this. He lay with his face against the deck and he was not a Starwolf any more; he was a hurt puppy.

"Do you like it?" asked the voice of Vlanalan. "Like it, strangers. For there is more, much more."

A terrible hatred grew in Chane. He had been hurt in conflict and borne no grudge, for getting hurt in conflict was natural and if you did not want to risk it you avoided conflict entirely. But this relentlessly applied, scientifically calculated torture, the cool taunting voice, made him feel a hatred he had never felt for an enemy before.

Chane nursed his hatred. It fought back the pain. He hated Vlanalan and all the Qajars. He would pay them back for this. And that meant that he must survive. . . .

Survival first, and then revenge.

Survival . . .

They must get away from here before the Qajar ship came.

He fought to clear his mind of the daze of agony. He could never make it to the controls; he knew that. The force that brought the pain to his nervous system had stunned all his motor centers. And there was no hope in Dilullo, who sagged in the pilot chair and seemed not to breathe.

Was he dead? *Oh God, did I bring him here to die?* What, then?

Gwaath rolled on the deck, howling. The feeble twitching had become a wild flailing. His hands and feet struck the deck plates.

Chane looked at him through pain-misted eyes.

The force that tormented them was attuned to human bodies, human nerves. Gwaath was humanoid but not human, bred of a different stock. He was suffering but he could still move, still howl.

Chane waited until Gwaath's head was near him, beating on the deck like a hollow gourd. He had to wait so that his croaking whisper, which was all the voice he had, might be heard.

"Gwaath. Gwaath . . . !"

Gwaath continued to roll and flail his hands about.

"The controls, Gwaath. Throw us . . . out of orbit. Escape . . ."

He kept saying *controls escape Gwaath,* or trying to say them, but the words did not seem to have any shape to them and Gwaath seemed to be beyond hearing in any case. Then it seemed to him that Gwaath's rollings and flounderings and howlings were moving him closer to the control board, and he watched, thinking how strange everything looked when you saw it through your own blood and tears, forced red and watery to burst the eyeballs. The distorted shape of Gwaath moved in the redness. . . .

Howled suddenly.

Flung itself sprawling upon the control board.

The voice of Vlanalan said something shrill.

The ship roared out of stationary orbit. And the agony was doubled, tripled.

The unseen net was reaching now to kill them before they could get away.

X

Chane was surprised to wake up. He had been sure, when that last blast of unspeakable pain had knocked him into darkness, that he was dying.

He still lay on the deck. The fiery anguish had left him, but all his nerves crawled and twitched and rippled with the memory of what had been inflicted on them. For the moment he was incapable of movement; his motor centers appeared to have burnt out. He wondered if it was permanent.

He lay there and thought of the Qajars. How clever they were, with their sensor rays and their probes of pain. How ruthless they were, those calm-faced lovers of beauty, delighting in tormenting those who might threaten their treasures, drawing a man's soul out of his body as slowly as possible and enjoying his suffering. He could imagine what would have happened to the three of them if the Qajars had got them on their world.

Gwaath bent over Chane, bringing his furry face down close and looking inquiringly at him with red-shot eyes.

Chane made a great effort of will and spoke. One word.

"Dilullo?"

"Not dead," said the Paragaran. "But not awake, and nothing wakes him."

"Help me up," said Chane.

Gwaath did so. He did it three times before Chane finally got his legs under him and stayed up, with only a little help. The big Paragaran still looked a bit groggy but otherwise was nearly normal. His humanoid body had endured that last blast of agony pretty well. But Chane himself knew that he had been very near to death when the scout sped out of orbit and out of range of the force.

And Dilullo?

He thought, when Gwaath helped him to the pilot's chair, that Dilullo was dying. His eyes were closed, his pulse slow, his whole body slumped and shrunken. Dilullo was a lot older than he, Chane thought, and the thing had hit him harder.

He had Gwaath open down one of the folding bunks and carry Dilullo back and put him in it. Chane sat down for a few minutes, trying to get his shocked nerves back to normal so that he could move without falling over.

The scout was in overdrive. Gwaath had set a course

toward Rith, but the course was not quite correct. Chane reached out a shaking hand and reset the course. After a time he got unsteadily to his feet and went back to Dilullo.

Dilullo still lay with his eyes closed, his breathing spasmodic, his face gray. Little shudderings of his limbs and body were evidence that his nervous system was suffering the same aftereffect that Chane had felt.

Chane massaged nerve centers, while Gwaath looked back anxiously from the pilot's seat. Finally, to Chane's immense relief, Dilullo opened his eyes.

They had a dull, glazed look, and when he spoke his voice was thick and slurred.

"We burned our fingers that time, didn't we?" he said.

"We did," said Chane, and told him how Gwaath had got them out of orbit.

"Well, we did right to bring Gwaath along," said Dilullo. "I guess we're lucky to get out of this one with our lives."

Chane said bitterly, "I'll show the Qajars some bad luck if I can ever get back at them. Damn them!"

"I've seldom seen you so angry," Dilullo said. "Usually you just take it as it comes."

"You didn't get the full blast of it," said Chane. "You passed out quick. But I got it all, and I'll pay them for it when the time comes."

"Forget it," said Dilullo. "Think instead about what's going to happen when we come back to Rith empty-handed."

Chane thought about that, all the long time it took the scout in overdrive to cross the Spur. He could see big trouble ahead and he did not like the shape of it at all.

But he worried more about Dilullo. Dilullo had not completely snapped out of it. His face was thin and drawn, his body still occasionally twitched as the nerves remembered their torture. Chane thought he would lose these aftereffects in time but he was not sure. And his own bitter hatred for the Qajars, for the cool voice that had mocked them as it applied the agony, deepened.

When they dropped out of overdrive and came in to Rith, they were surprised to find a watery sunshine on its daylight side. But beyond the black stone city, vast masses of dark cloud brooded sullenly, promising more tempest for this storm-ridden planet.

Rith officers met them and escorted them to the barny palace of Eron. Nothing was said except a few politenesses until they reached a chilly stone room where Eron sat. The bantam-sized red ruler looked at them accusingly.

"You didn't get the Suns," he said.

"Ah, so your men have already searched the scout and called you," said Dilullo. "No, we didn't get them. We were lucky to get away alive."

"For your lives I care nothing," said Eron angrily. "Nothing, you understand? What concerns me is your failure."

Dilullo shrugged wearily. "You can't win them all. The Qajars were just too much for us. You said they wouldn't full-scan, and they did."

He told what had happened and the cocky little ruler strode back and forth nervously, his tough face getting darker and darker in expression.

"It comes to this," he said finally. "You used a Rith scout. You tried to deceive the Qajars and failed. Suppose the Qajars ask me how you got that scout?"

"Tell them we stole it," said Chane.

Eron glared at him. "You think it's that simple? You still don't comprehend all the powers of the Qajars, even after they showed they could handle you like children! Suppose they find out you're here and demand that I surrender you to justice—their justice?"

"Are they likely to do that?" asked Dilullo.

"I don't know," said Eron uneasily. "Nobody knows what the Qajars are liable to do because nobody knows the extent of their powers, how far they can see, what weapons they can wield. I know one thing: I don't want them as enemies, and I don't want to lose them as profitable customers in trade."

"What you're leading up to," said Dilullo, "is that if the Qajars ask for us, you'll throw us to the dogs."

"If necessary," said Eron harshly. "Only if necessary. But you will have to stay here until I'm sure the Qajars are *not* going to demand you."

"Fine," said Dilullo. "A fine loyal partner you make."

Chane said nothing. He had expected this.

"Nothing here will harm you," Eron went on. "I've given a small wing of the palace to your men and they've been quite comfortable. So will you be."

"In other words, we're prisoners till you find out which way the cat jumps," said Dilullo disgustedly.

"Yes," said Eron. "You will go now."

He gave an order in his own incomprehensible language and one of the officers and four armed Rith came forward. Chane noticed that they were armed, not with stunners, but with lasers.

It was no time to make any resistance, he decided. He and Dilullo went along with the Rith as meek as milk. They went up through stairs and corridors, poorly illuminated, where the gentle blue faces of the old race had, not been painted over. The faces looked down at the captives as with vague pity.

The men halted at a guarded door. A Rith officer searched Chane and Dilullo very efficiently, taking everything they had in the pockets of their coveralls.

Then the door opened. The ugly, grinning little red man gestured to them with a sort of mock politeness. They went through and the door clanged behind them.

There was a long ill-lit corridor and there were doors off it. Some of them were open, and from one they heard the sound of voices. They went that way.

Most of the doors opened onto small sleeping rooms, but the one from which the voices came was a bigger common room. The windows of all these rooms were mere ventilation slits, too narrow to admit anything larger than a cat.

Janssen sprang up from the group that was sitting around and drinking Rith liquor in the common room.

"What do you know?" he exclaimed delightedly. Then his face fell as he looked them over. "You didn't make it, did you?"

"We didn't come within a mile of making it," Dilullo said. He went over to the table and sat down in a chair, and Sekkinen poured him a drink of the fiery liquor from a slender flagon.

Gwaath reached for the flagon, and it was a measure of Dilullo's weariness that he did nothing to stop him. The big Paragaran tilted the flagon and drank with a gurgling sound and put it down and wiped his hairy lips.

"We were knocked silly," said Gwaath.

Chane was not all that tired but he sat down. He saw Bollard scrutinizing Dilullo's worn face by the light of the lamps that were set in brackets around the walls.

"You know what, John?" said Bollard. "You look like hell."

"So would you, if you'd been through the wringer we went through," said Dilullo. He drank again, and then he told them all about what had happened.

"It was a nice idea," said Dilullo. "Real nice. Only it didn't work. And now we're in a bad jam."

They all sat and thought about that. Nobody said anything for a while. Gwaath reached for the flagon again, but Chane got up and took it from him and poured himself a glassful of the liquor. Then he handed the vessel back to the Paragaran, who emptied it in a long gulp.

"We've done a lot of things," said Dilullo. "We've pulled it out of the fire a good many times when nobody thought we could. But no matter how good a man is he's going to fall on his prat sooner or later. This is where we did."

"Then we kiss the whole job goodbye?" said Janssen.

"What do you think?" asked Dilullo.

Neither Janssen nor anyone else had an answer to that. After a moment, Sekkinen said, "Then the only thing left is to make a break and get the hell off this planet and go back to Earth?"

Chane spoke up. "It won't be easy. We might break out of this place, but when we landed at the starport I noticed that they've got enough guards around our ship to hold onto it. Also, there are heavy lasers trained on it."

"I don't know," said Dilullo. "I just don't know."

Bollard looked at him keenly. Then the fat Merc

got up and said decisively, "One thing for sure. We're not going to do anything tonight. You need some rest."

A tremendous banging of thunder punctuated his words. Lightning flared outside the window and thunder rumbled again, and then there was the crashing sound of rain.

"Give us this day our hourly storm," muttered Janssen. "What a planet."

"Come on, John," said Bollard. "I'll show you where you can sleep."

Dilullo got up and followed Bollard out of the room and down the corridor, a man in a daze. Chane went with them, not liking the look of Dilullo and afraid he might keel over at any moment.

Dilullo made it into one of the rooms and onto a bed. He was asleep before he hit it.

Bollard bent over him, loosening the neck of his coverall, taking off his shoes, putting a blanket over him. From the little window came the hiss of the rain and the turmoil of the storm, and Chane thought, *Janssen's right; what a world!*

Chane went out of the room with Bollard. But in the corridor, after he had closed the door, Bollard suddenly stopped. His round fat face was not at all good-humored and moonlike now. It was dark and angry, and he reached out his hand and caught the front of Chane's coverall and pulled him closer.

"Are you happy, Chane?" he demanded.

"What the devil are you talking about?" Chane demanded.

Bollard did not let him go. "Are you satisfied, now that John is about half dead from the job that you thought up for him?"

Chane began to understand. "So that's it. The job

is blown, we're in a mess, and now you're crying because it was my idea. Look, you're all grown men. You could take it or leave it when I proposed to go after the Singing Suns. You took it."

Bollard nodded. "We did. And none of us are crying. But with John it was different. He'd retired. He had money. He was going to build him a house and live easy, after all the hard knocks he'd taken across half the galaxy."

A dangerous light came into Bollard's small eyes. "But you wouldn't let him be. You had to drag him back into space. You went after him and talked him into it, and now where is he? His money's gone, he's half dead, and he's liable to be all dead before we're through. And you did this to him, Chane!"

Chane's anger surged up and he raised his arm to send Bollard crashing back into the wall.

He did not do it.

He could not answer the accusation.

It was all true.

XI

IN THE MIDDLE of the night after the third day of his imprisonment, Chane lay unsleeping. A dark and bitter anger had been growing in him.

His anger was directed partly at himself. He had done an evil thing, by his own code. To a Starwolf, a debt was something that must be paid. He owed Dilullo his life, yet how had he repaid him? By cajoling him back into space, to be subjected to an agony that had now made him only a shadow of his former self.

And why had he done this? The others might think

76

it was because of greed for the great reward offered for the Suns, or because of sheer lust for adventure. But Chane knew the truth. He knew that it was the chance to get back to the Spur that had driven him. His nostalgia for the world of the Starwolves had become such that even to look at Varna and its sun from a distance had drawn him like a magnet. He had talked the others into this reckless mission chiefly for that.

And John must have suspected it, thought Chane, *but he never said a thing.*

But he also had another anger, one mixed with bitter hatred, and that was directed at the Qajars. Those calm-faced, beauty-loving men who had savored such quiet delight in torturing Dilullo and Gwaath and himself.

If I could make them pay, he thought. *If I could smash in there and loot away their treasures and leave them wailing . . .*

It was just his anger and hate speaking, he knew. There was no way to do that. They were prisoners here on Rith, and if the Qajars demanded them they would be turned over, to be tormented until they died.

The Qajars had weapons of unguessable capacities. There was no power in the Spur able to beat them down, and forces from the main galaxy were not allowed to come into the space of the Spur worlds.

No power in the Spur? Chane's pulse suddenly leaped. There was one power that could do it . . . maybe.

Varna.

The Starwolves would go anywhere, and fight any fight, for loot. They would have raided the Qajars' gloomy world long ago if they had dreamed of the immense loot there.

And what if he, Chane, told the Starwolves about that loot . . . and proved it to them? Ah, what then?

Chane uttered a mirthless whisper of a laugh. It was a fine idea. Fine, except for just one thing: if he went to Varna, he would be killed before he could tell anything. The clan of Ssander still hungered for his death.

He dismissed the idea that had been born of anger and desperation. He lay in the darkness, watching the tiny window that was lit to a white flare every few minutes, listening to the distant thunder as another of the incessant storms approached. Between the rumbles and bangs he could hear the heavy breathing of Van Fossan and Sekkinen and Janssen, who shared the sleeping room with him.

But his wild idea would not go away. He kept thinking about it, even though he knew it was all folly. How could he land on Varna without having to face Ssander's clan one by one in single combat, as Starwolf law demanded?

Gradually, a possible way crystallized in Chane's mind. It was only the shred of an expedient, and it was almost sure to fail. But it *might* be done.

Chane sprang up silently from the bunk. He would not think about that possible expedient any more. If he did he would see its hopelessness. No, he would act upon it. Any action was better than being cooped up here waiting for doom.

He would act now. This minute.

But how escape this prison?

The walls were of blocks of solid stone. The windows were too small to get through. There was only one entrance and Riths armed with lasers stood outside it. This was, obviously, a detention wing.

Chane thought and thought. He could see only one possibility, and that seemed a pretty thin one.

Don't think! Act!

He took his coverall and turned it inside out. The stout cloth had an inch-wide tape border over all the seams. The tape was not cloth, though it looked like it. It was a woven plastic stronger than anything except steel. And it could be detached.

Chane detached it, and it came away in one unbroken length. It was doubled, and when he had undoubled it, it formed a thin rope over thirty feet long.

Bad fixes were habitual with the Mercs, and over the years they had worked up a good many little things like this tape to help get them out. Chane now proceeded to another of those things.

He turned the coverall right-side out again and put it on. Then he unsnapped the broad button that held the flap of the upper right-hand pocket. The button was a miniaturized ato-flash with good intensity for its size, but with a capacity of less than a minute's duration.

Not enough, thought Chane. *Not nearly enough.*

He moved silently around the room, picking up the coveralls that belonged to the three sleeping Mercs and robbing them of their buttons.

Then Chane went quietly out of the little sleeping room and down the corridor to the common room. There was no provision for sleeping here, nothing but a few bench-like chairs, so the room was deserted.

Lightning flashes from the advancing storm lit the room. Chane went to the window. He removed the plastic shield that kept rain out, and by the light of the recurrent flashes he studied the window carefully.

In the stone-block wall, one block had been omitted to make this opening for light and air. Not the thinnest man could wriggle through the small opening. But his examination convinced him that there might be another way.

Chane took one of the miniature ato-flashes and turned its minute flame of force upon the thick mortar around the block immediately beneath the opening.

In forty seconds the flash went out, its charge exhausted. He used another one, and another. Then he studied his handiwork by the lightning flares.

The mortar was deeply cut all around the block. But how deeply? Enough?

There was only one way to find out. He got his arms out through the small opening of the window and took a grip from the outside on the block.

Bracing himself, he put all the Starwolf strength Varna had given him into a mighty heave.

The block moved inward, with a grating noise that sounded as loud as the crack of doom to Chane's ears. Luckily, one of the frequent rolls of thunder from the approaching storm masked it.

He had pulled the block no more than an inch inward, but now that he knew the mortar was cut through he had no further doubts. He kept heaving and pulling in little jumps, each time waiting for a clap of thunder before he did it.

The block finally came clear. His muscles were now so numbed by effort that he almost let the block go crashing to the floor of the room. He managed to prevent that by pressing with his body against the block, holding it against the wall and slowly easing it to the floor.

He stood up, panting and sweating. The small window, now that the block beneath it was also out, had become just big enough for an average-sized man to wriggle through if he held his belly sucked in and didn't breathe.

And then what? Chane thought of an old Earth proverb that Dilullo used: *Out of the frying pan into the fire.*

He shrugged. Maybe it would prove so. But he wasn't even out of the frying pan yet.

He moved one of the heavy benches, as silently as he could, to a position just beneath the opening. He got up on it and stuck his head out and peered downward. Some of the windows below showed light, and he remembered the way they had come well enough so that he was able to tell which one was a window of the big throne-room where Eron had talked to them and shown them the tridim pictures.

It was not directly beneath him. It was the second window to the left, two levels down.

Chane estimated distances by the lightning flashes. He did it as carefully as he could, for everything depended on his estimate.

When he felt sure, he took his long tape and tied one end to the heavy bench. About two-thirds of the way to the other end he tied a loop big enough to get his foot into. Then he dropped the tape out of the window.

There was one more thing to do before he went. On a table lay the deck of cards which the Mercs had been allowed to keep, alone of all their personal possessions, and with which they beguiled their captivity.

Chane took a card and, with the tongue of his belt-buckle, scratched white letters on the colored back. Only a few words, telling Dilullo that he was going in an attempt to help them get out of this, and that he would be back.

No more than that. Another Merc than Dilullo might read this first. He put the card down conspicuously apart from the pack and then went back to the window.

By the flashes he tried to see if there was anyone in the wooded grounds of the old palace. He could see no one and he hoped he was right because he was about to show up as clearly as a fly on a white wall. He twisted his shoulders into the enlarged opening.

He thought at first he was not going to get through. He backed off and tried again, letting one shoulder go first. This time he made it, barely. He grabbed the tape, drew out the rest of his body, clamped his feet on either side of the tape, and then slid slowly down until his feet felt the knot of the loop.

Chane got his right foot into the loop. He would have liked to pause for another breather but he was too conspicuous hanging up here in the glare of the ever-increasing lightning-flashes.

He began to swing himself, gripping the tape to pull it in and then letting go of it. He swung parallel to the wall and so close to it that his fingers, gripping the tape, rasped painfully against the stone. Chane swore but kept swinging. He thought with grim amusement that he would be a damned outlandish sight if anyone saw him.

Lightning washed the wall every half-minute now. The thunder had become deafening. He hoped that the close approach of the storm would have discouraged anybody from being out of doors.

He swung wider and wider until at last he was swinging just below the edge of the window he wanted.

Chane gripped the stone sill with his fingers and then slowly drew his head up to look inside.

The window was a good-sized one, there being no need for precaution as in the detention wing. The plastic pane was closed against the coming tempest.

It was the right room, the big barny stone room gauded with tasteless trappings that was Eron's idea of an audience chamber. It was softly lighted, and two of the runty, red-skinned men bearing lasers strolled two and fro in it.

Chane had expected that. It seemed that Eron kept some of his treasures in this place, and he would not leave them unguarded.

He waited, hanging onto the windowsill, until both guards had their backs to him. Instantly Chane drew himself up until he crouched in the deep window-opening.

He braced his feet against the stone. With all the Varnan speed and strength he possessed he hurled himself forward, and the light plastic pane went flying into the room.

The two Rith guards swung around. They were fast but no one was as fast as a Starwolf, and Chane reached them as they first began to raise their lasers.

He hit one man with a clean punch, saw him drop, and kept on without stopping his movement. The second man had got his laser almost to the firing position. Chane's fist opened, became a hand, grabbed the barrel of the laser and slammed it upward with tremendous force into the guard's face. It hit the man's forehead like a hammer. He let go his end of it and fell down.

Chane examined them. They were both unconscious. He tore strips from one of the florid hangings and carefully bound and gagged them. It seemed a waste of time, but he could not kill these men. He would be leaving Dilullo and the other Mercs captive here, and if he killed any Rith, John and the others would suffer for it.

And there was no question, there never had been any question, that he could take the others with him. One man, himself, alone, might make it out of the palace and to the spaceport without being caught, but not the whole mob of them. If his plan worked, and worked in time, he might save them. If it did not . . .

No use worrying about them now. Chane sprang to the cabinet from which Eron had taken the tridim pictures.

It was locked, and the lock was strong and good.

A swiftly-gathering roar came from outside as the rain arrived. Chane set his teeth and forced himself to work calmly and deliberately with the lock. He had to have those pictures if his mission was to have any chance of success. They were the only means of proving at Varna that his whole story of the Qajars and their treasures was true.

He was clever with locks; nearly every Starwolf was. He found the combination, opened the door, and a moment later had the thick little plastic pictures in his hand. He stuffed them into his pocket, ran to the window, and started to slide down the rope to the ground.

The rain smashed him with solid masses of water. He had seen Rith rain before, God knew, but he had never felt it. Its pile-driver blows knocked him down along the rope like a toy monkey on a string. He hit the ground with a bang.

Chane had thought that the rain would be an ally, keeping people inside and helping to hide his movements. He found out now that with an ally like this he did not need an enemy.

The rain pounded him, trying to inlay him into the muddy ground. He breathed incautiously and got solid water up his nose. He snorted it out, shielded his nose with one hand, and finally managed to get to his feet and stand shakily erect under the downpour. It was like standing under a waterfall.

He could see almost nothing. Only the fact that the wall of the palace was against his back told him it was there at all. He clung to it, orienting himself, he knew the direction in which the spaceport lay but he was afraid that when he let go of the wall he would lose all sense of where he was.

Still, he could not stand here shivering. He had to make his try. He fixed his mental compass reading and started walking.

A man could not go far in this. It was a battle to stay on his feet, a battle to move at all. Sometimes he went on all fours until some chance shelter let him rise again. He was blinded, deafened, dazed, strangled. The only thing that kept him moving was his Starwolf pride. *A man would give up,* he kept saying to himself, *but not me, not a Varnan.*

He bumped into a stone wall. He was in a street now, and it seemed, as far as he could guess, to lead in the direction he wanted. He staggered along it like a blind man in the stunning rain, one hand trailing along the building walls of the street side.

He was never able to tell later how long he had struggled forward. When the guiding wall ended he knew that he was out of the small capital of Rith. But which way now?

There would be lights at the starport but he could

not see them. He could not see anything. He thought he might as well take a chance and go on in what he thought was the right way.

He did, and got nowhere except to a growing realization of failure. His head was so dazed by the impact of the downpour that when it began to lessen he did not at first realize it.

The rain slacked off until it was no more than a heavy cloudburst on Earth. And he caught the watery gleam of lights not far away to his left.

His knees went weaker still with relief. It was the starport, only a few hundred yards away.

And now he had to hurry. If the storm slackened any more he would be caught flat out. He took a deep breath and began to run.

He went straight onto the starport, running. He might be tripping a warning beam, but it had not seemed to him that the Riths were as hipped on security as all that, and anyway, he had to take the chance.

He heard no alarms. And suddenly out of the sheets of rain there loomed a vague but familiar outline.

Their Merc ship, with its typical Terran eyebrow bridge. He could not see anyone around but he sheered away from it even so. He knew the ship was guarded; the guards would be inside now, sheltering from the storm.

The Merc ship gave him his bearings. He angled away, passing the vague bulks of other ships, until he came to a much smaller craft: the scout in which he and Dilullo and Gwaath had made their ill-fated journey to the Qajar world.

He had thought it would still be here, knowing that it would take at least a couple of days to service it.

He opened the airlock and went inside, ready to attack if anyone was there.

Nobody was. There was no particular necessity to mount a guard here, and it had not been done.

Chane closed the lock and got the lights on. He shook himself like a half-drowned dog, and got busy.

The scout had been serviced. Good. He got into the pilot's chair, sitting with runnels of water dripping from him to the deck.

He took the scout up and away from Rith as fast as it would go, giving not a damn for any precautions. He came up into clear space and set his course. Far away but bright, ahead of him, shone the tawny star of Varna.

He had tried to be a good Earthman with the Mercs. But he was not a good Earthman.

He was a Starwolf, and he was going home.

XII

HE WOULD KNOW, he thought, within the next twenty-four hours which it was to be—life . . . or death.

The scout had dropped out of overdrive and the great golden sun blazed huge before him, and the blue and copper ball of Varna came around it toward him, as though to welcome him. But what kind of welcome would he find there?

He knew the watch that was kept and he was expecting the challenge which at a certain moment came from the communicator.

He answered, "Morgan Chane, coming into Krak starport, in a Rith scout."

There was a long moment of silence and then a shocked, astounded voice said, *"Morgan Chane?"*

"Yes."

Another silence, and then the voice said, "All right. Come on in . . . if you want to!"

Chane smiled grimly. He might not last long on Varna but it seemed that he was going to be a sensation while he did.

He drove the little scout downward and it seemed to him that he fell swimming in a cataract of the tawny golden sunshine. Of a sudden he felt unbeatable, unconquerable. He knew that this was only the euphoria of coming home and he laughed at it in his own mind, but he could not help it.

It was spring on Varna and the great arid planet had a surface of pale green instead of the usual burnt gold and brown. And there came up the metallic-looking oceans and the green lands, and finally the far-scattered sprawl of dull red stone that was Krak.

On the broad starport the neat squadrons of small, needle-shaped ships were drawn up, glinting in the golden sunshine. It was all as it had always been.

Only it was not. . . .

All the feeling of long nostalgia left Chane. He became wary and cold. It was all very well to come back home, but there were those at home who wanted very earnestly to kill him, and he must forget emotions if he was to live.

When he had landed and cracked the lock he stepped out into the hot dry sunlight. The heavy gravitation of Varna grabbed him and almost staggered him. He had been away from Varna for quite a time and he had to get used all over again to the drag which had so nearly killed him as a child. It reminded him tha he had no advantage here, that he was merely one Starwolf among many, and not the strongest.

He stood there beside the Rith scout, listening to the cracking sounds as it cooled.

Then he saw a man striding out toward him.

Berkt, he said to himself.

All of the Starwolves walked proud, but none in quite so tall and proud a way as Berkt. He was one of the greatest of the leaders, who had raided more worlds than Chane had seen.

He came closer, tall and mighty, the light golden down of his body hair glistening in the sun with only a leather harness to cover it. His slanted, uptilted eyes, pale as agates, bored into Chane's.

"I didn't believe it," he said. "I was seeing to the refitting of my ship, and I heard it, but I didn't believe it."

"Hello, Berkt," said Chane.

Berkt disregarded the greeting. He looked at Chane and he said, "Now understand me, Morgan Chane. I don't particularly care whether you get killed or not."

Chane nodded.

"But," said Berkt, "I feel I should tell you that almost the whole clan of the Ranroi, Ssander's clan, is on Varna right now. If you want to live, take your ship and go."

He added, "I think you know why I'm giving you this warning."

Chane nodded again. He knew.

Berkt was years older than he was. He had never particularly liked Chane, though he had had no particular dislike for him.

But Chane could remember the time when he was a small boy; when his father, the Reverend Thomas

Chane of Carnarvon, Wales, Earth, and his wife had still been living.

Two rather small people who had come to Varna as missionaries, to reform the wicked Starwolves. They had, of course, got nowhere at all. Nobody came to their pathetic little chapel except curious Varnan children. The mature Varnans just ignored them.

Except Berkt. He had not had the smallest shred of religion, any more than any of the Varnans had. But he was, even in those days, a leader of great courage and renown. And Berkt had seen courage in the slight, small figure of the Reverend Thomas Chane. This little Earthman, who with his wife was slowly dying from the heavy gravitation of Varna, but who would not give up, who would not go away, held to his mission until they both were dead.

The most unlikely of friendships, Chane had thought of it later. The mighty young Starwolf lord, and the frail little man who had come from Earth to preach. He could remember, from his boyhood, his father's glowing face as he talked, sitting on the bench in front of the little chapel, and with a tall young Berkt sitting beside him, gravely listening, not pretending to agree but never contradicting.

"You've got your father's courage," Berkt was saying. "And I see you have his stubbornness. What the hell are you doing on Varna?"

"It's a rather long story," said Chane.

Berkt said, "You don't have that long. You're a dead man if you don't go away."

"I am not going away," said Chane. "I have something to tell the Council."

"Fine," said Berkt, looking disgusted. "Well, I'll give you a drink or two before you're killed. Come along."

Chane walked with him across the starport. It was a long walk, because this main starport of Varna was a big one. For this was the home nest from which the falcon ships of the Starwolves raided out across the galaxy.

A roaring thunder echoed from the brassy heavens, stretching far away across the starport. Big, powerful machines were hammering and probing at ships that had come back from raids with wounds in their sides. Power units throbbed, raged, and sometimes coughed and died, as they were repaired and tested. Heavy truck-carriers rumbled between the ships, taking supplies. There was a deafening roll and crash across the sky as a squadron of five needle-shaped ships came in for landing after a test flight. . . . He knew it was a test flight from their formation and from the fact that none of them had scars on their sides.

There were hundreds of ships, thousands of Varnans, on this port, and all of the men were busy at their work. The work of the Starwolves was robbery, the far-flung raids across the galaxy that had made them famous and infamous, and they loved their work and toiled as industriously as bees to make sure that when they went forth on a job of stealing by force, none of their ships or equipment would let them down.

But the work slowed, almost stopped, where Berkt and Chane walked between the ships. Chane was, and always had been, a standout here, for his dark, compact form and his coverall garment were quite different from the gold-haired, harness-clad figures of the Varnans. They knew him when they saw him; there were not too many on Varna who had not heard about the Earthman Starwolf, and it seemed also that they knew what had happened to him, for they stared at him in incredulous wonder.

"They just can't believe," said Berkt, "that you were crazy enough to come back."

Chane shrugged. "I'll admit it must look that way to them."

Berkt looked at him curiously. "Where have you been all this time, anyway?"

"With the Mercs," said Chane. "They picked me up when I was about half-dead from the wound Ssander gave me, and I joined them."

"Then they didn't know that you were really a Varnan? They couldn't have known, or they'd have hung you."

"One knows," said Chane. "Not the others."

"I've heard of these Mercs," said Berkt. "Are they any good?"

Chane turned and looked at him as they walked. "They're not as good as the Varnans; they haven't got the Varna-bred bodies for it. But they're good. Good enough to outfox a Varnan squadron in Corvus Cluster."

They came out of the starport, and Berkt had a car. It was not like the cars of Earth, soft-riding and smooth and silent. It was a vehicle as tough as the Varnans themselves, and it went over the rough roads outside the starport—What? A Starwolf labor on roads?—with a jolt that Chane remembered and enjoyed.

They went up and down the rocky, craggy hills. Varna was a poor world, which was why its sons, when they had attained starflight, had gone out to loot the rest of the galaxy. The golden sun was declining and its rays lit the harsh landscape. Down there below the hills was the city, Krak, but there was not much of it. A great market-square with buildings of dull red stone around it, but the Varnans, who had the freedom of the stars, did not much enjoy living crammed together.

The lords of Varna, such as Berkt, had their keeps and strongholds of stone set well apart from each other, preferably on the tops of the rocky hills. It was the lesser ones and the young men who lived in the city, as Chane had once lived in the stone barracks down there.

The car jolted on and approached a stone wall. They went through its gateway, and before them was the rambling pile of reddish stone that was Berkt's home.

A tall golden woman came out to greet the noisy approach of the car, and then she forgot her husband to stare at Chane.

"Nshurra," he said, and smiled.

"The little Earthman," she said. "Oh, no, it can't be."

There had only been two people on Varna who could call Chane a little Earthman without a fight. Both of them were women, and Berkt's wife was one of them.

"Did you bring him back here to be killed?" she demanded of Berkt.

"Bring him back?" said Berkt. "He *came* back. He's tired of living; he wants to die. At least that's the only reason I can see."

Nshurra came and grasped his hands. "Chane, we thought you were dead. Everyone thought so."

She had always liked him. Chane had always thought that her liking had been born of pity, for she was older than he and could remember him when he had been an Earth-descended child struggling to move, to breathe, against the crushing gravitation of Varna. He could remember Nshurra picking him up and helping him along, when he was a child. But always when no one else could see, so that he might not lose face and pride.

They stood under the stone portico, with the tawny blaze of the sun almost level on their faces. Chane, feeling for the first time a real sense of homecoming, turned to Berkt.

"May I kiss her?"

"If you do, I'll break you in half," Berkt said casually.

Chane smiled, and kissed the golden cheek. He went with them into the place, and it was cool and shadowy and as he remembered it. Presently they sat on a balcony and watched the sun go down. They drank the Varnan wine, wine so strong that it was said it would kill anyone but a Starwolf. It did not kill Chane, but made his head ring as though with golden bells.

"All right, Chane," said Berkt. "Tell me."

Chane told him. Of Dilullo, ill and trapped on Rith along with his comrades, and the fault all Chane's. Of the treasure of the Qajars. Of his hopes to get part of that treasure, and with it to pay Dilullo the debt of life he owed him.

He told him everything, except one thing. He did not tell of the Singing Suns being in the possession of the Qajars.

Berkt was silent for a while, and then poured more wine. The sun had gone down and the great ragged blaze of the Spur stars was across the sky. The smell of Varna came up to Chane, and it brought old memories.

He wished that he had been born to be Berkt. How would it be to sit here and look at the stars, and know that you would presently go out and raid them of riches, and return, and drink your wine, and know yourself one of the lords of Varna? He had thought that one day it might be so, with him.

Berkt finally broke the silence. "I'll tell you something, Chane. Nshurra was always fond of you, because she helped you when you were a child. I never admired you."

"I know that," said Chane.

"Then, know this," said Berkt. "For throwing away your life—and almost certainly that's what you're doing—to help your friend, for that I do rather admire you."

Chane took the little tridim pictures out of the pocket of his coverall . . . all except the one that showed the Singing Suns. That he had put into a secret pocket.

A viewer was brought, and in the dusky room the glories of the Qajar treasures were shown.

"How could we ever have missed a hoard like that!" Berkt exclaimed.

"They're clever people, the Qajars," said Chane. "Extremely clever, and very subtle, and a little mad. They've got practically a world of radite and they've used it to pay thieves to bring them all the things they set their hearts on. They've also used it to keep themselves hidden, and to set up powerful defenses. It was one of their defenses we ran into."

"And you want revenge for the torture they subjected you to? Is that it?"

"For that, and for what they did to Dilullo," said Chane. "But also, I want very much to get my hands on some of the Qajar treasure."

"And so you came here with those pictures, to drum up a Varnan raid on the Qajars," said Berkt.

Chane nodded.

"It's not a bad idea," said Berkt. "Not bad at all, except for one thing. The one thing is that you won't live long enough to see this through."

Chane smiled. "That remains to be seen."

Berkt refilled his glass. "Chane, I'd like you to tell me something: How did you come to kill Ssander? You two were good friends."

"I thought we were good friends," said Chane. "We'd grown up together here. He used to bat me around when we were boys, because he was stronger and wanted to prove it. Once in a while, I'd manage to bat him around. All very natural."

He drank and put his glass down. "We raided Shandor Five, and Ssander was sub-leader. We did well, and Ssander took a sub-leader's share of the loot, and that was all right with me. But then, when it was all divided, he saw a jewel he fancied in my share, and he said, 'That's mine, too.'"

Chane poured himself more of the wine, and drank, and Berkt watched him with his piercing eyes.

"I thought it was like when we were boys together on Varna," Chane said. "I struck him. I batted him back, and said, 'You've had your share.' And he looked at me and said, 'You damned Earthspawn, you struck me.' And he grabbed his laser and shot me in the side. I shot back, and killed him. And then his brothers were coming, and there was nothing for me but sudden death if I stayed, so I jumped into one of the ships and took off."

Berkt nodded, after a time. "I thought it was something like that. You know, Chane, you're a bit unfortunate in feeling like a Varnan but looking like an Earthman."

A communicator inside the room purred softly, and Berkt went in and spoke briefly into it. When he came back he said, "That was Chroll calling—you remember him? He tells me that several men of Ssander's clan are at the starport, watching your ship. Just watching, to make sure you don't go away in it."

He added grimly, "You're in the trap, Chane."

XIII

THE BLUE-BLACK night skies of Varna lit to silver and then to silver-pink, as the two different-colored moons chased up into the sky. They lit the road that went down into Krak, and Morgan Chane followed it, finding a certain satisfaction in the solid way his heels hit the ground. He thought that Varna was a harsh mother, big and bony with rock and dragging at its children with its heavy gravitation, but still it was his mother world.

The air was cool, with a faintly metallic smell to it that came from the not-too-distant ocean that ran up onto the stony beaches in long, furious tides. Down there ahead of him the warm and ruddy lights of Krak beckoned, and all was as it used to be. Or nearly so.

Chane left the road by the first bypath, and continued to work his way down toward the city by little-used paths, and then into the city by obscure streets well away from the lights and noise of the great market-place. In that market, rich goods looted from all over the galaxy were bought and sold; there were always many people there, and it was no place for a hunted man.

If I can slip around to the west and reach the Hall, he thought, *I may just pull it off.*

If the clan of Ssander—the clan-name was the Ranroi, after a revered ancestor—caught him before then, it was all up and his gamble of coming to Varna would have failed.

He was not, of course, afraid of being suddenly shot

down. The clan of Ranroi had great honor, and he would be given the formal challenge and the fight would take place at the appointed place, in the way that was perfectly legal on Varna.

"They know you're in my house," Berkt had said. "They won't bother you here, of course, for that would be starting a feud with me. But they'll wait patiently, right from the first, for you to come out. You might just as well try it now."

Chane had thought so, too, and here he was, slipping along a dark little street which he knew perfectly well, with the great stone bulk and lighted windows of the young men's barracks a few blocks away on his left.

He heard from one window the sound of voices raised in a chorus. The Starwolves sang in a way that made you think of lions singing. He could not distinguish the words but he knew the tune of it and had many times himself sung the song, which was a highly disrespectful one about a great Starwolf lord who was constantly rushing off on foolish raids because he could not endure to stay home with his shrewish wife.

Chane grinned, and slipped on. He had learned these dark streets very well indeed, in times past when he and Chroll—and, yes, Ssander—had stayed out later than barracks law permitted, and had had to return unseen.

Two or three times he saw people moving ahead, and each time he went down a crossway, not ducking stealthily but staggering and throwing his arms around as though very drunk, so that the difference in his figure might not easily be perceived.

He finally stood behind the Hall.

The big, square, and unlovely mass of stone was the only center of government the Varnans of this region had. They were a highly individualistic people who wanted as few laws as possible. A Council of twenty decided all issues beyond the individual. The Council was unique in that, though its members were chosen by vote, only Varnan men who had taken part in at least five raiding missions were allowed the vote.

Chane thought that it was unlikely that any of the Ranroi would be here. They would not be expecting him to come to the Hall, not having as yet any idea why he had come to Varna.

Still, he went around the more shadowed side of the massive building as carefully as a hunting cat. He reached the corner of the front facade and peered around it.

Nobody was in front of it.

Chane went fast, then, to the tall open door. It was always open, and there was always an official here to hear appeals.

The official sitting now at the wide desk was old, for a Varnan. Few Starwolves, by the nature of their hazardous profession, lived long enough to get gray, but this old man had white in his hair and shaggy eyebrows, making him look like an aging tiger.

The old man said nothing, but his upslanted eyes narrowed slightly as Chane walked toward him. He knew perfectly well who Chane was—everybody in Krak knew about Chane—but he nevertheless asked.

"Your name?"

"Morgan Chane,"

"You have completed five missions?"

"Many more than five."

The old Varnan opened a section of the desk and touched studs. Presently a card popped out. He looked at the card.

"Verified," he said. "What is your purpose?"

"To make an appeal to the Council," said Chane.

The cat eyes narrowed a trifle more. "The nature of your appeal?"

He thinks I'm going to ask Council to have the Ran roi restrained, thought Chane. *As though the Council would ever take away a clan's feud-right!*

"My appeal is for a hearing in which I will propose something that could enrich all fighting Varnans," said Chane.

The old man's eyes widened a little in surprise. But he reached for a book and opened it, and wrote briefly in it.

"Your right of appeal is legal and is granted," he said. "You will be notified when Council will hear you."

Chane bowed to him, with the respect of a young fighting-man to an old one with also a touch of *To hell with you!* in it. He thought that the shadow of a grim smile came onto the old Varnan's face, as he turned and walked out of the Hall.

He was outside, his appeal had been granted and witnessed, and now what? Back to Berkt's? No, not yet.

Violet lightnings had begun to play in the west, out over the sea. Varna had thunderstorms that made the thunderstorms on Earth look childish, but Chane, from long familiarity, decided that this storm would not come inland.

He walked the streets now, not caring who saw him. Varnan men and women stared at him, and to those he knew, he bowed. They greeted him, with a sort of startled air.

He had walked like this, in the lights and the crowds of tall Varnan people, in years gone by. He had realized quite well in those days that he was behaving like a cocky bantam, simply because he was a bit smaller, and, on the whole, a bit weaker than these tall golden folk.

He walked like that now, not caring much where he walked. And then he found himself in quieter streets, and when he began to realize where he was, he realized that old-time habit had betrayed him and had taken him to a place where he had not really wanted to go.

A quiet street, with rather small houses. He wanted to turn around and leave it, but somehow he could not quite do so. He did not stride arrogantly now, he plodded. And his slow steps took him to a small, old house that had snarling masks carved on its rainspouts, and that had next to it a vacant lot with a few tumbled stones lying about in it.

The distant lightning flared, and washed out the light of the silver and pink moons. Chane went into the lot and looked around.

His father and mother had lived in the small house, and on this empty lot had been the chapel, long fallen to ruin, where the Reverend Thomas Chane had preached.

Chane thought, *Just like Dilullo. Does everyone have a vacant lot, a lost something or someone, in their past?*

He walked to the back of the grass-grown space. His father and mother had been buried behind the little chapel where they had striven so valiantly for their creed.

The violet lightning far out over the ocean flared and he saw the two small tombstones. They were clean and well cared for, and he could even read the letter-

ing, for it was in the fire-stone that was Varna's hardes[t]
mineral.

"The Reverend Thomas Chane, Carnarvon, Eart[h]
. . . ."

And he remembered the old man in bleak, wind[y]
Carnarvon who had said, "The Reverend Thomas w[as]
a fine man and a strong preacher. I do not doub[t]
that he converted many out on that distant world befor[e]
the Lord took him."

No, he had not. The Reverend Thomas had con[n]
verted no one. But he had made at least one frien[d]
Chane had no doubt at all that it was Berkt who ha[d]
kept the graves cared for. He remembered the funera[l]
and he remembered Berkt taking him, a boy trying [to]
restrain his tears, and shoving him into the door of th[e]
place where young Varnans learned their skills, an[d]
saying to him, "Go in there, and find out whether you'[re]
fit to be a Varnan or not. It's not what your fath[er]
would have wanted, but there's nothing else for yo[u]
on Varna."

Well, there was no use at all in thinking about [it]
now. But even Starwolves mourned their dead.

He heard a sound and swung around. There was [a]
man near him, a tall, dark figure.

Then the distant lightning flared again and he kne[w]
the man.

It was Harkann, the oldest of Ssander's brothers.

XIV

"I THOUGHT you would come here," said Harkann.

He was years older than Chane, and he was one [of]
the Starwolf lords, not as great a one as Berkt, but [a]
famed leader of raids.

He towered over Chane, and in the shadows Chane
uld see the livid scar across his forehead from an old
ound, where the Varnan down would never grow again.
nderneath that scar, the slanted eyes seemed to glow
the dusk as he looked down at Chane.

"I'm glad you came back to Varna," said Harkann.
"ery glad."

Chane smiled. "I rather thought you would be."

"I have told all the Ranroi not to challenge you,"
id Harkann. "I have wanted the pleasure of this
for myself."

Chane said nothing. After a moment, Harkann added,
t will be tomorrow, then? You know the place . . .
is still the same one."

Yes, Chane knew the place, the rocky gorge not far
tside Krak where feuds could be settled fairly and with
danger to anyone else. And Harkann would be there,
th his weapons, and if Harkann did not manage to
l him in fair fight, it would be the turn of Thurr,
e other brother of Ssander, to try to do so. And if Chane
led Thurr, then one by one any others of the clan
Ranroi could challenge him. It was a big clan, where-
Chane had nobody at all: his only kin on Varna lay
neath the two fire-stone markers.

"I have claimed the Council right," said Chane.

Harkann's head jerked with astonishment. "The Coun-
right? For what reason?"

"I have come to Varna with something for the Coun-
to hear," said Chane.

Harkann was silent for a moment, his big catlike
dy hunched forward as he glared at Chane. Chane
uld guess his frustration.

No feud could be pressed against a man who had
aimed the Council right, until the Council had heard

that man. It was unbreakable law, designed to preven
one litigant from challenging and killing another lit
gant before the Council could hear the case.

"It's a trick," Harkann said. "But it won't save yo
Chane. You murdered Ssander—"

Chane interrupted sharply. "Ssander tried to murde
me. And he damn near succeeded. I only drew m
weapon after he had used his on me."

"Murder, self-defense . . . it doesn't make one b
of difference to us of the Ranroi!"

"I never thought it would," said Chane. "But I wa
the record straight."

Harkann said between his teeth, "The record w
very soon be closed for you, Chane."

He turned away. After a moment Chane left th
place also but he went another way.

He headed westward, toward the place where th
sea came nearest Krak. There, on a cliff above th
ocean, towered one of the lordly castles, arrogant
the light of the flying moons. As he went forwar
toward the building, he could already hear the thu
derous booming of the great tides beating against th
base of the cliffs.

A woman came out into the moonlight from whe
she had been sitting on a carven stone bench benea
a tree.

Chane smiled. "So you were so sure I would con
that you were waiting for me, Graal?"

"You were mad to come back to Varna at all, Chane
she said. "Do you know that right now the Ranroi a
looking for you?"

"I know," he said. "I've met them. But there's a d
lay in their plans, for my Council right."

He stood, admiring her. Graal was taller than

was, and her splendid, golden-down covered body was very little concealed by the garments she wore. With her glowing chatoyant eyes, she looked like a beautiful panther.

"Why did you come back, Chane?"

"To see you, of course."

"Liar," she said. "Tell me."

He told her. She shook her head. "But after the Council hears you, you'll have to fight the Ranroi, one after another."

"I have an idea about that, too," said Chane. "But we won't talk about that, but about you. Berkt says you are not yet married."

"I am not," said Graal. "I like fun and men too much to tie myself to any lord yet."

"I know." He nodded. "I used to get quite furious with you about that."

"And you're not furious now?" She moved closer to him, in a way he remembered. "Perhaps you have met out-world girls more attractive?"

"One," he said. "On a world called Arkuu."

Graal burst into laughter, and then put her arms around him and kissed him. It was something like being kissed by a tigress.

"That's my little Earthman, always trying to make me feel jealous."

Chane grinned. "It's true."

"Then you shall tell me about her."

They walked beneath the trees, in dappled pink-silver moonlight and shadow. Graal seemed already to have forgotten her worry for him. She was a fine, generous, merry-hearted girl, but she was a daughter of Varnans, and a Varnan's business was fighting.

The sea boomed, and the wind had hints of metallic-tasting spray in it. The moons glided on and their shifting radiance poured down, and it was good to be again on the world of his youth and with Graal's arms around him.

"I'm sorry if I'm interrupting," said a man's voice.

Graal only laughed, but Chane turned angrily. Then his anger left him as he saw the young Starwolf who stood with an amused look on his handsome, reckless face.

Chane went to him and gripped his arm warmly. "Chroll!" They had been comrades on many a raid, and both remembered.

"Would you mind if I take him with me, Graal?" asked Chroll. "I'm trying to get his neck out of the noose into which he has run it."

"Then take him," said Graal. "I don't want my little Earthman hurt, if it can be prevented."

She gave Chane her mocking smile as she said that, but he only smiled back at her, and then went with Chroll.

As the car started down the hillside, Chroll talked fast. "I heard about your claiming the Council right, Chane. But that won't protect you for long. Old Irrun, the head of the Ranroi, is one of the Council and will see that you get a hearing fast. And after the hearing, you'll have no Council right to protect you."

Chane said, "I've got an idea that might still restrain the Ranroi after the hearing."

He told Chroll his idea, and Chroll said that he did not think much of it.

"Irrun will try his best to quash any such proposal as that," he told Chane. "And if he succeeds, then what? You'll have to face one after another of the Ranroi until one of them kills you."

He swung the car from the base of the hill, toward the lights of Krak.

"I can get you off Varna, Chane, but it will have to be tonight. If we can get unnoticed into my ship . . ."

"No," said Chane. "I bring no other man into my private feud. That's the way I was taught here, and that's the way it will be."

"Damn Ssander!" muttered Chroll. "I never did like him, though I know you did."

"Besides," said Chane, "just escaping from Varna is not what I want. I came here to do something, and just to go away without even trying to do it would be a stupid waste of time."

"Berkt told me of your plans," Chroll said, after a moment. "I can't say that I blame a man for loyalty to his comrades." He added, after a moment, "By the way, Chane, don't say anything to Berkt of my offer to get you away, will you? He wouldn't consider it quite honorable."

"You're still as much in awe of Berkt as when we were boys, then?" said Chane, laughing.

"Yes, I am. And so are you."

Chane did not deny it. Chroll asked, "Do you want to go back now to Berkt's?"

"What would you want to do if it were your first night on Varna for a long time?"

"I'd want to raise a little hell," Chroll said.

They did. They went to the huge tavern by the marketplace that was the favorite drinking place of the Starwolves.

The place roared and blazed. The red-colored lights did very little in the way of illumination, but they were sufficient to enable a man to find his glass. None of the great Starwolf lords were here; they were far too proud and dignified for that. But the junior officers, the fighting men, the men Chane had known, were here in great numbers.

They hailed him in good friendship. Obviously the word had got around that he had returned to Varna. Three of them, who were of the clan of the Ranroi, got up and somewhat ostentatiously left. But nobody paid much heed to them. These young blades didn't give a curse for feuds, but they had raided with Chane, they knew him as the poor little Earthman (none of them dared use that phrase to his face) who had had a hard time growing up on Varna but who had made it; they liked him, and they bought him wine.

The strong wine went down and Chane's head rocked and rang, and he thought, *This is not very well advised, but damn it, it's part of what I came back to Varna for*, and he drank it down and went on from table to table.

Talk, talk, good talk, talk about the last raid to the Hyades, talk about Sarn and how he got himself into a lot of trouble off Deneb: he thought he had a fat lot of loot just sitting there waiting to be picked up, and did he get a nasty surprise! Talk about Aranso, and how he ran right through the triple crown, the three stars whose gravitic tides were murder, but he did it. And Chane bought a large cup of wine for Aranso and complimented him, and Aranso insisted on his sharing the cup. Aranso was rich with loot, and in a drunken, happy mood, and at this moment he loved Chane like a brother.

"And where have you been, Chane? What have you been doing with yourself?"

Chane was pretty exhilarated by now, and enjoying

it greatly, and he poured himself more wine and stood on a table.

"Do you really want to know?"

"Of course we do!"

"I have been with the Mercs," he said. "Nearly all of them Earthmen."

"Back to your own, is that it, Chane?"

Chane drained the cup, and then looked at them and said gravely, "You are my own, you miserable, misbegotten sons of Varna."

Laughter and cheers. Most of them were getting a bit drunk by now, and they enjoyed the insult.

"What are Earthmen like, Chane?"

Chane considered. "They're stupid, for one thing. They have all sorts of vague, cloudy ideas about morals and laws and doing good for people."

"Like when they first came to Varna and taught our people how to build starships?" shouted someone, and the whole great room rocked with laughter.

That was a famous and favorite story on Varna. How the Earthmen, who had discovered the principle of the stardrive—rediscovered, really, since it had been known ages ago by the race who had seeded the whole galaxy with humanity—had come and innocently offered to show the Varnans how to build starships, so that they might engage in honest trade in the galaxy.

And how the Varnans of that day had demurely said, yes, they would very much like to have starships so that they could engage in honest trade and be good men. And, having thus gulled the Earthmen, they had learned how to build starships, and had been the raiders and robbers of the galaxy ever since.

"Yes, they're stupid," said Chane. "They clog up their

minds with nice ideas that somebody thought up. But, my brothers—"

"Yes?" said someone.

"They are a goddamn tough lot," said Chane. "They can't move in space the way we do; their bodies aren't up to it, for Earth isn't a heavy-grav world. But . . . they are tough."

He thought, as he spoke, of Dilullo and Bollard and Sekinnen and the others, and of the things they had done together.

"I was on Earth," said Chane. "I went back to the place where my parents came from. And there was a young man there who taught me a song, and the song he taught me was an old Earth battle-song. That song might tell you what the men of Earth are like. Do you want to hear it?"

"Sing it!" they cried, and Aranso sent him up another cup of wine, and he drank it off and now his head was really ringing, but nevertheless he still remembered the song that tall young Hayden Jones had taught him in the little bar at Carnarvon.

He sang it, the old war-song of the men of Harlech, and the Starwolves listened fascinatedly, and then they began to sing it too, the great, tall cat-eyed golden-furred men who scourged the stars, singing of Saxon bowmen and Saxon foemen as though they had just come out of the dark marshes of Wales with their swords and spears in their hands.

The idea made Chane stop singing to laugh. And as he stood laughing among the roaring chorus, a hand plucked his knee, and Chroll was there, offering him another cup of wine.

"Having a good time, Chane?"

"I am having a good time."

"That's good, Chane. That's very good. Make the most of it. For old Irrun worked fast, and the Council will hear you tomorrow, and it may be your last good time for a while."

XV

THEY WERE the greatest of the Starwolf lords, and they sat like kings behind their wide table at the side of the dusky stone hall.

Chane, standing facing them, thought fleetingly, *Dilullo would call them a royal bunch of robbers.*

From one point of view that was true, for raiding and robbing were the life of Varna. These nine men represented the greatest Varnan clans, but also they were famous for the great Starwolf raids they had led in bygone years.

Khepher, who had led the great raid on the Pleiades that had brought home such loot as Varna had never seen before; Somtum and Yarr, who had hit the throne-world of Canopus, looting for the first time the royal treasury of a system so huge and powerful that it had never feared attack; Berkt, sitting there and looking as though he had never seen Chane before, who had struck halfway across the galaxy to lift the legendary Terbium Ten and fight his way home with them again; Vonn and Martabalane and Munn, who had taken the treasured jewels of Betelgeuse Four away from their spidery owners by a triple-play feint and attack that was a classic of Varnan history; Hof, who with only twelve ships had bagged the richest convoy in the galaxy's history; and Irrun, who had privateered all along the north-zenith edge of the galaxy and had come home with ships heavy with plunder long after he had been given up for lost.

They were all looking at Chane, and the regard of Irrun was a piercing one. The head of the Ranroi clan was a massive man well past middle age, who sat with his wide shoulders hunched forward as he stared at Chane. He had been Ssander's uncle, and he would be the main difficulty in the way of Chane's proposal.

Khepher, who had the seniority of the Council, spoke formally to Chane.

"Very well, Morgan Chane. The Council will hear you."

Chane braced himself. If he failed here, Dilullo and the other Mercs might never leave Rith.

"My appeal is for the right to present a plan that could bring vast riches to Varna," he said.

They looked surprised; Irrun's eyes narrowed and he looked as if he was going to interrupt. But Khepher said, "You have leave to speak."

Chane pointed to the compact projector-device he had brought with him. "Can I, before speaking, show a few tridims relative to what I will say?"

Khepher nodded.

Chane turned on the device, with its controls set to reproduce a three-dimensional image of life size.

The first Qajar treasure room sprang into vivid, almost solid-seeming glory in the shadowy hall: jewels heaped up in golden jars, jewels woven into tapestries, weird statuettes that were each cut from a single blazing gem . . . all with such reality that the astonished Starwolf lords, except for Berkt, leaned forward as though they would grasp these things with their hands.

"What foolery is this?" snarled Irrun.

"I am showing you the treasures of the Qajars," said Chane. "There are more."

He changed the tridim and another of the incredible treasure rooms came into being. And as he showed room after room, the slant eyes of the Starwolves gleamed with lust for plunder.

When the last tridim had been turned off, Khepher leaned forward. "Where are these things?" he asked. "*Where?*"

"On the planet Chlann, of a people called the Qajars," said Chane. "It lies not far outside the Spur."

"The whole galaxy would have rung with the news of such a treasure, if it existed!" said Irrun.

"The Qajars," said Chane, "are a clever people. Oh, very clever. They have gathered together the most beautiful and costly things in the galaxy, having paid thieves to steal them. They have kept all this secret and have kept their world secret, and very well defended. I know; I nearly died trying to get to their treasure."

He paused, and then added, "I can guide you there. I can lead a Varnan squadron through their defenses, although I cannot guarantee that there will be no losses. I will do this, if I may have my pick of any single item of the Qajar treasures."

"You are bold to come and make terms with the Council," snapped Khepher. "Is there anything else you want, perchance?"

"One thing more," said Chane coolly. "Council right to protect me, until the squadron returns to Varna."

Irrun leaped to his feet, his face raging. "A trick!" he roared. "This man killed my nephew and has incurred the feud of my clan. He asks the Council right so that he can escape our rightful revenge."

Chane stared at him, as though not in the least impressed by Irrun's position and fame.

"To escape your clan-feud," he said coldly, "I needed only to remain away from Varna."

Berkt laughed. "You will have to admit that young Chane has a point there."

Irrun said fiercely, "It is well known, Berkt, that you had a friendship with this outworlder's father!"

Khepher's voice rose sharply. "There will be no bickering between members of the Council! We are here to listen to the man Chane, and then later to decide."

He turned his attention to Chane. "Describe what you know of the defenses of the Qajars."

Chane did so. He stressed that he was the only one who could lead a Varnan squadron with any safety whatever into that cluster of dead suns and worlds.

"These so-called Lethal Worlds that you describe," said Khepher; "you went safely between them and back again. Could you lead an attack squadron that same way?"

Chane shook his head. "Not possibly. The Qajars just did not think it worth while to use such huge weapons against my small scout. But against a squadron, they would use them. My suggestion is that we sacrifice a number of old ships, unmanned and on automatic pilot, sending them in ahead of us to blow enough of the Lethal Worlds to make a passage."

He went on rapidly: "The Qajars have powerful radiation defenses; I felt them. Anti-radiation helmets should help us there. And they have a fairly powerful squadron of battle cruisers, though none of them heavies. But I feel we could handle those, if we could get through the Lethal Worlds."

"The strategy would have to be debated later, by those fit to do so," said Khepher in cold reproof. "But if we smothered the Qajar defenses, you could lead us to the treasure chambers?"

"I could," said Chane, and added in his mind, *All except one, where I'll never lead you. I'll give you one of the biggest hauls Varna ever had, but not the Singing Suns.*

The examination went on, others of the Council flinging sharp questions at Chane. These were men who had a lifetime of raiding behind them, and who knew about every danger interstellar space could hold, and they were not going to take anything for granted.

"It has not been explained," said Irrun sharply, "how these Qajars could have acquired sufficient of the highly rare radioactive substances that would be required to convert dead planets into their Lethal Worlds."

"My information from Eron," said Chane, "was that there are tremendous deposits of radite, one of the rare substances you mention, on the world Chlann. It is the source of the Qajars' wealth, with which they've bribed thieves to steal treasures for them."

Chane added, "Eron felt sure the Qajars are a bit mad. They've nested there behind their defenses, gloating over their treasures and avoiding direct contact with most of the galaxy. If anyone approaches them uninvited, they kill him by torture. I say that this thief-spider nest should be broken into, and their treasures taken by more suitable owners—namely, the Varnans."

Some of the Council lords smiled at that: it was exactly the kind of talk to be expected from a cocky young Starwolf.

"The matter will not brook sudden decision," Khepher told Chane. "It must be further examined. The tridims must be gone over by experts to make sure they are not fakes. Our records concerning that cluster must be examined to see if they contain any contradiction to your statements."

Chane bowed. Khepher concluded, "You may go for now. You will in time be notified of our decision. Until then, you continue to have the Council right."

Chane would have liked to say more but this was an arbitrary dismissal, so he bowed again and left the Hall.

Two nights later he sat in the moonlit gardens behind Berkt's keep, drinking wine with Chroll and Graal and Nshurra. He knew very well that Nshurra had never liked Graal and her free-and-easy ways, but she had been smilingly hospitable to her.

For two days Chane had awaited the Council decision. In those days he had had a fine time reliving old days with Graal . . . and nearly getting drowned by her when she held him under water as they swam the great tides of the beaches beyond Krak.

"Relax, Chane," said Chroll. "It'll be decided soon, one way or the other."

"What do they think of Varnans on that old world of Earth, Chane?" asked Nshurra. "You said you were there."

"Savages," said Chane. "Wild, hellroaring savage robbers of the whole galaxy." He looked at Graal and added, "They say the Varnan women are even fiercer than the men."

Graal promptly threw her wineglass at him, and he ducked just fast enough to let it go past his ear.

From far away at the distant starport beyond Krak,

there was a series of three twanging sounds and three bolts of light flashed up into the sky.

Chroll smiled. "A small party of very young Varnans, going out to try their luck. They'll probably come back empty-handed. But you remember, Chane?"

"I remember," said Chane. "Very well."

There came the jolting grind of one of the heavy Varnan cars ascending the hill, and Chane tensed. He tried not to show it.

None of them spoke until the grinding stopped, and presently Berkt came around into the garden.

"Well?" said Chane.

"I won't keep you in suspense," said Berkt. "After all this argument, the Council has decided to sanction the raid on Chlann, and the clans have pledged in all some seventy ships."

Exultation soared up in Chane. He could almost feel his hands on the Singing Suns.

"But before you get too happy about it," came Berkt's dry voice, "there is a condition attached to the sanction. It was attached by Irrun and his supporters on the Council, otherwise they would veto the raid."

Chane stiffened. "A condition?"

Berkt nodded. "Irrun's nephew Harkann commands the raid. And, as pilot, you go with him in his ship."

"So the Ranroi are not going to let me out of their grasp?" muttered Chane.

A rage grew up in him. Damn the Ranroi and their feuds! He would go with Harkann, but if one of them had to perish, it was going to be Harkann.

XVI

A GREAT HORN bellowed brazenly across the city Krak. And at that signal, other mighty horns took up the clamor, echoing and re-echoing off the stone walls until the whole city was buffeted by waves of brassy sound.

In long ago days the Varnans had been a fighting race, and the battle horns had sounded when the clans went out against each other. And though centuries had gone by, and though they had become highly sophisticated in the technology of star travel which Earthmen had unwisely taught them, the old custom remained and when a Varnan expedition set forth to raid for loot, the great horns all sounded.

Out from the red stone buildings broke the brilliant flags of the different clans. With cheers and waving of hands, the tall golden people along the streets honored the cars that were filled with fighting men, and that rolled and jolted away in the direction of the starport.

Chane, riding in one of the cars, thought, *On Earth, they'd do this for a defending army going forth, but never for a band of pirates going for loot.*

But it was the way he remembered it, and the brazen roaring of the great horns sent a hot thrill through him as it always had in the past.

There was a brightness in the eyes of the Varnans riding with him. They might be going to sudden death between the stars, but there would be excitement and fighting and maybe a shipful of rich plunder to bring home, and this was the way a Varnan liked it.

It made Chane think of the very first time he

had gone out on a raid, how he had tried to conceal his excitement as the horns bellowed, how he had tried to look cool and haughty and as unexcited as the veterans around him.

To the devil with nostalgia, Chane thought suddenly. *Nostalgia will get me killed.*

No raid he had ever gone on would be as dangerous for him as this present one, and he had better stop dreaming and keep alert every moment.

The hot golden sunlight poured down on the cars as they rumbled out onto the starport and between the long lines of needle-shaped ships. Beside the ship that was starred with the symbol of the leader, the figure of Harkann towered above a group of captains. Harkann gave Chane an icy look, but did not otherwise greet him.

"You all know where the dropout point will be," he said, and they nodded. Chane had calculated that dropout point, and experts in stellar navigation had confirmed it. Harkann went on, "You know the order and timing in which we'll drop out; you have the full schedule. So there's nothing more to talk about."

The captains went away, all except Harkann and Vengant, who was his second officer. They turned and went into the symbol-starred ship, and Chane followed them.

The ships of the Starwolves were small ones, with a crew of eight to ten each. The fighting men of the ship gave no greeting to Chane. They were all of the Ranroi clan, and knew him. Vengant took the controls, and Harkann and Chane the chairs behind him. They looked out through the broad bridge screen, and nobody said anything.

From far away they could hear the brassy echo of

the horns of Krak bidding them farewell and good loot
ing. Then a new sound began.

It was less a sound than a vibration, and it grew
until the tarmac under the ship was quivering with it
A deep and awesome thunder, the thunder of the firs
division of ships as their power units came on.

"Time," said Harkann curtly, and as he spoke, the
first division started skyward, with a lightning-bolt
sound of splitting atmosphere.

Thirty needle-ships, heading halfway up the zenith
But these were not proud Varnan craft. They were old
corroded, their sides scarred by battles out in distant
space from which they had limped home long ago
They had been furnished with enough repairs and
power to get them into space again, and had been
manned by skeleton crews. They were the expendables
the sacrifice to deceive the Qajars. With them were
five sound ships to take off the skeleton crews when
the moment came.

The roaring thunder of their takeoffs died away
and Harkann sat silently watching the chronometer
Finally he said into the communicator, "Second Divi
sion, five minutes to offworld."

The chair in which Chane sat began to quiver a
the power units back in the stern compartment began
their muted roar. The five minutes went by.

An explosion of power hurled the ship skyward
and smashed Chane deep into his chair. His guts con
tracted agonizedly, and he felt his vision darkening
as an unseen fist battered his head, and he thought
startledly, *I've been too long away from Varna; I can
take this many gravs now!*

Then his belly muscles tightened up, and his vision
cleared, and he knew that he had not lost the strength

that the painful years of childhood on Varna had given him, that he could still endure.

The ship kept rising on an acceleration schedule that would have paralyzed an Earthmen. That was why the Starwolves were so hard to beat in space. The heavy gravitation of massive Varna had bred into them a strength and resistance that made them able to take G's which no other spacegoing race in the galaxy could take.

Chane took it, and liked it. This was the speed at which he had been used to traveling in space until the time he forsook Varna. The slow speeds of the Merc ships had sometimes seemed intolerably sluggish to him.

They went away fast from Varna. Out in the brilliant sunglare, on either side of the flagship and behind it, shone bright, winking little points of light that were the other ships of the squadron. Starwolf forces kept tighter formations than ordinary men could dare, since they could if necessary alter course with sudden changes of speed and direction that would crush the guts out of an Earthman.

From the golden glare of Varna's arrogant sun they went out into the blackness and the starshine, driving headlong toward the predetermined drop-in point.

"Time," said Harkann, and Vengant hit the controls and went into overdrive.

The vertiginous feeling of the fall into extra-dimensional space came and went. Without a pause, the ship hurtled on, and all the ships that were behind it.

And still none of the Ranroi had said a word to Chane.

Chane remembered what Berkt had said, before he left Varna. Chane had been saying goodbye to Chroll, who had signed long before for another raid and was not going against the Qajars, and who was unhappy about it.

"Don't feel too badly about not going with Chane," Berkt had grimly advised Chroll. "Wherever Chane is on this job, there's going to be the worst danger."

"You don't mean that the Ranroi will try to kill him out there?" Chroll had exclaimed. "No, they wouldn't. . . . He has Council right until the raid-squadron returns."

"There's a good many of the Ranroi I don't like, but they're not dishonorable," Berkt said. "They—or most of them—wouldn't break Council right. But there'll be fighting out there, and Harkann can give Chane the most dangerous spot in it without violating his right."

Later, after Chroll had left, Chane had looked at Berkt and had said wryly, "Thanks for the encouragement."

"You know it's true, don't you?" said Berkt, and Chane nodded.

Then Chane hesitated. Something bothered him.

"You've been a good friend to me, Berkt," he said.

Berkt shrugged. "Partly for your father's sake, and Nshurra's."

"I haven't told you the whole truth," said Chane. "It's not that I've lied about anything, but I omitted a bit of the truth."

Berkt said nothing, waiting.

"The thing I'm after on the world of the Qajars," said Chane. "The one item of treasure which, by the Council terms, I'm permitted to select for myself. Between us, it's the Singing Suns."

Berkt's upslanted eyes opened wide, and a look of incredulity crossed his cruel-planed, haughty face.

"But the Suns were broken up!" he exclaimed. "After Morrul and his clan stole them from Achernar, Morrul sold them to Klloya-Klloy on Mruun, and Klloya-Klloy broke them up and sold them to several buyers."

"The several buyers were all agents of the Qajars," said Chane. "It was their trick to keep down the price of the Suns."

Berkt stared, and then suddenly broke into a burst of homeric laughter.

"That's the damnedest thing I ever heard! Then that's what you and your Merc friends came to the Spur for?"

Chane nodded. "To get the Suns and collect the two million credit reward for them when we return them to Achernar."

"*Return* them?"

Chane said defensively, "Earthmen are queer fish, Berkt. Even the Mercs, who are pretty tough, won't do anything that's against their particular ideas of honesty. I'll admit it seems pretty foolish to me."

"If Harkann and the others see the Suns, they won't much like your taking them," warned Berkt.

"I know," said Chane grimly. "But the Council agreed that I could take any single treasure-object I wish. And I'm going to do just that . . . if we get that far."

"Which is a big if," Berkt said. "Harkann's a good raid leader, whatever else he is. But from what you told me, you're going up against some pretty nasty stuff. Well, good luck!"

Remembering that now as the ship flashed on in overdrive, Chane thought he would need the luck. Now and then he caught the eyes of Harkann, cold and deadly, watching him.

It did not exactly frighten him, but all this inimical

123

silence on the part of everyone began to bore him. When he had finished a trick at the navigation instruments, he went back to the tiny bunk room and stretched out.

He wondered what Dilullo and Bollard and the others were doing, if they still lived. He grinned as he thought what they would say if they could see him now, out with the Starwolves.

Well, the devil with worrying, he thought. *I've made my gamble and I'll follow through with it, and there's no use thinking any more about it.*

They went on, angling across the whole width of Argo Spur. They stood their tricks, and checked the ship weapons, and ate and slept and watched the simulacrum viewscreen that showed their squadron passing between the nebulae and stars.

A tenseness grew in them as they neared the edge of the Spur. Beyond it the screen indicated empty space, the great ocean that washed the shores of the galaxy.

And out in that space showed the dark cluster that Chane remembered, the little cluster of many dead suns and worlds in the heart of which the Qajars had their stronghold.

There came a time when Harkann said, "The first division, right now, should be *here*," putting his finger on the screen on a point two-thirds of the way out to the dark cluster.

Chane was sure that they would be right where Harkann had indicated. They had to be, to make the whole attack plan work.

Starwolves, contrary to general belief in the galaxy, did not rush bullheaded into an attack when they raided. It often looked that way, but actually the dreaded Varnan raiders planned their major raids on a finely-calculated schedule.

It had to be that way for a raid to succeed. The Starwolf squadrons were never very big. Given time, almost any planet they hit could bring up overpowering forces against them. So the Starwolves never gave them that much time. They dropped out of overdrive at the precise right moment, used their unmatchable speed in space to make a lightning swoop, grabbed their loot and went away again as fast as they had come.

Chane felt the familiar feeling of tenseness, excitement and eagerness he had always felt when a raid mission neared its climax.

He thought, *Dilullo would be disappointed in me. After all his efforts, I'm still a Starwolf!*

When they had approached almost to the edge of the dark cluster, as shown on the simulacrum, Vengant said sharply, "Dropout time for One!"

Harkann, studying the screen, nodded silently. Some distance ahead of them in space, not far from the actual edge of the dark cluster, the fleet of thirty old ships that were to be sacrificed would at this moment be dropping out of overdrive.

Chane could visualize it. The skeleton crews of the old ships, now that they were in normal space, would be swiftly setting the controls on their automatic, prediagramed courses. Then those crews would be picked up by the five sound cruisers that had gone along with Division One for that purpose.

The chronometer showed a figure, and Vengant said, "Time."

"Drop out," said Harkann.

They came out of overdrive next moment, with the dizzying, spinning sensation you never got used to.

On the viewscreen, now that they were in normal space, they could see far to their left the vast coast of the galaxy, sweeping away in cliffs of stars. The tarnished plume of Argo Spur was behind them. Ahead there was only the darkness of space, in which the dark cluster could not yet be seen visually.

But the radar screen showed the little cluster sharp and clear. It showed five blips outside the cluster, the ships that had taken off the skeleton crews. And it showed thirty other blips, racing at highest speed toward the cluster and soon to enter it.

Harkann spoke into the communicator, to the whole squadron.

"Be ready for the signal."

It seemed to Chane, as it had always seemed to him at this penultimate moment before an attack, that as the squadron waited it was quivering to be unleashed.

XVII

THE THIRTY SACRIFICE SHIPS flew fast toward the dark cluster. The ships were not bunched together, but were spread out in a broad line. The course to be followed through the dark worlds and dead stars of the cluster had been carefully programed for each one of them.

"If your Lethal Worlds exist, we should soon see some evidence of them," Harkan said to Chane.

They peered at the viewscreen, which had now been set to give a close-up view of the cluster.

"Nothing," said Vengant, contemptuously.

Blinding light flashed from the viewscreen as a

small, dark planet exploded into a colossal flare. The flare of force engulfed several of the robot Varnan ships, but the others raced on.

"It seems," said Chane, "that the Qajars keep a good watch on their monitors. And that the sight of Varnan ships has upset them."

Another body in the cluster, a big planet that swung far out from its dead and ashen primary, flashed into a parsec-wide flare.

"Seven more of the robots got it," said Vengant. He began to swear. "Who are these crazy people, anyway, who explode worlds as a weapon? It's sheer madness."

Chane shrugged. "They've got the worlds to spare. . . . This cluster is just a graveyard of dead suns and planets, with no life on any of them. And they've got the radite. A big charge of it, when it's set off, transforms a great mass of the planet into unstable atomic compounds, and it blows. It's easy for them."

Another mined planet blazed up, and then two more almost at once. All the dead suns and icy worlds of the dark cluster sprang into visibility in the unthinkable glare that was the pyre of planets.

"All thirty of the robot ships gone," reported the man at the scope.

"How near did they get to Chlann?" demanded Harkann.

The man punched a key, and then read off the figure.

"Pretty near," muttered Harkann. "But there might be a few more explosive worlds yet."

Chane shook his head. "Too near Chlann for that, I think. They would hardly want a backblast from their own weapon." He added, "Well, the robot ships have made a path for us through the Lethal Worlds. Are we going in?"

"We'll go in," said Harkann, and spoke the signal, and the whole Starwolf squadron dashed forward in a long, narrow column.

It was a poor fighting formation if the Qajars came out to fight, thought Chane. But only a narrow column could follow the gap made by the robot ships through the Lethal Worlds. And maybe that gap wasn't wide enough, maybe they would catch it in a planet-flare; but if that was so, they would never know what happened, so why worry?

They had put on the anti-radiation helmets that had been prepared at Varna, and Chane thought that they all looked oddly like ancient soldiers. But the helmets should keep out the worst of that mind-shattering attack weapon the Qajars used. He hoped.

The Starwolf column flashed into the cluster, following exactly the middle of the path that the sacrificed robot ships had taken. *The old Starwolf swoop,* thought Chane, *that all the galaxy feared.* But they might have bitten off too much, this time.

A hellish flare blotted out the whole universe on their right. A small planet had gone to glory there, but when their dazzled eyes recovered, they saw on the radar screen that the column had not been touched and was driving ahead.

Now other dead worlds and moons let go, and all space seemed filled with the gigantic flares. The circuits of the ship faltered, lights went out, the craft rocked and went dead and then picked up again, but all the time their roaring momentum kept them going in.

It was like running a gauntlet of world-destroying fires, thought Chane. Harkann sat like a rock, looking doggedly at the viewscreen, his massive shoulders un-moving.

He's my enemy and I'm probably going to have to kill him, thought Chane, *but he goes into battle like a Varnan.*

Shaken, quaking and shuddering, the Starwolf ships rushed on. Dead planets far too distant to harm them sent up their mighty flares as they exploded.

Chane thought that the Qajars must be afraid indeed of the Starwolves, to try to frighten them back with this holocaust of worlds. But it took a good deal to frighten a Varnan.

The last flares fell behind them, and their stunned eyes began to recover.

A needle of pain went through Chane's brain. It was like the time when he and Dilullo and Gwaath had been tortured, but not a tenth of that agony. It gimleted into his head, and seemed to twist and turn.

Some of the Ranroi crew had uttered exclamations, and Vengant was swearing. Harkann had half risen from his chair, and then he turned and looked at Chane with a question on his hard face.

"This is one of their weapons," said Chane nodding. "The helmets keep most of it out, but not all. We'll have to stand it."

"We'll stand it," said Harkann harshly. "But curse people who use such a weapon."

"They're clever, the Qajars," said Chane. "I'm hoping that soon we can make them pay for their cleverness."

The squadron rushed on toward the dark world that still was not visible to them. But now Harkann gave an order, and smoothly the squadron shifted from the long column to a new formation, which looked like an irregular swarm. There was nothing at all random about the casual-looking formation: every Varnan ship had its place in it.

"*Damn* this thing that gets into your brain!" said Harkann, shaking his head.

"Be grateful you've got the helmet on and aren't getting the full blast of it," said Chane.

The probing finger of pain in his skull made him remember the ordeal that he and Dilullo and Gwaath had gone through, and his lust for vengeance sharpened.

"Will they come out to fight?" demanded Harkann.

"I think they have to," said Chane, "when they see that neither the Lethal Worlds nor this pain ray is stopping us."

"They're coming now," said Vengant, and pointed to the radar screen.

Harkann and Chane studied the screen tensely, estimating the blips on it that now moved toward them.

"At least eighty ships," said Harkann. "Coming on in a concave formation. Figuring to box us in and give it to us from all sides."

"*Very* clever," said Chane. "But they haven't fought with Varnans before."

And he and Harkann both smiled grimly.

The swarm of Starwolf ships kept going straight ahead, and the Qajars half-moon formation flew toward them, so that the Varnan swarm would be caught between the horns of the semicircle, and be the target of concentrated fire.

They went on, and were actually between the horns of the Qajar half-circle, before Harkann rapped an order to his captains.

"The left horn. Up shields. All right, let's take them."

The whole Starwolf squadron suddenly turned sharply left. The turn was an impossibly abrupt one, for anyone but Varnans. Even though Chane expected it, and had braced himself in the chair in which he sat at the controls of a missile-launcher, the blood drove into his head and the pressure crushed him as with a giant hand.

The Qajars had indeed never fought Varnans before, and the swiftness and speed of the swerve took them by surprise. Before they could alter formation, the Starwolf ships were swarming around the cruisers in the whole left horn of the formation.

Two or three Varnan ships attacked each one of the Qajars, having here a local numerical superiority. The missiles began to flare and Qajar ships went up in destruction as their shields were overloaded, before there was even any firing back.

Chane kept the radar of his launcher locked onto a Qajar ship that was in plain sight against the stars. Two other Varnans were pumping missiles at it, and the strain became too much for its shields. The Qajar ship blew, and they turned to another prey.

"Hit them! Hit them before the others form up!" Harkann was shouting to his squadron.

The whole middle and right horn of the Qajar fleet was milling confusedly. They could not loose missiles at the Starwolf ships without hitting their own ships that were at death-grips with the Starwolves.

"Faster! Don't give them time!" Harkann cried, as Vengant drove their ship down toward a Qajar craft already engaged with a Varnan cruiser.

The vault of space was dancing with missile-flares, and Chane saw that the Qajar ships of the left horn were already mostly destroyed. The unexpected swiftness and savagery of the Varnan attack had taken a deadly toll.

Even as their immediate enemy's shields failed, and their missiles got through to it, Vengant gave a yell from where he sat at the controls.

"Harkann, look at them! The others!"

Chane turned to glance over his shoulder at the radar screen, as Harkann swung also to see it.

The remaining two-thirds of the Qajar force had not come into any formation. Suddenly, without any attempt to form an attack pattern, the whole formless mass of Qajar ships flung itself headlong toward the Starwolves.

"They must be crazy, to attack without formation!" exclaimed Vengant.

Chane remembered that Eron had said the Qajars were more than a little mad, and now he believed it. Only a sudden maniac fury could have impelled them to such an unplanned attack.

"Crazy or not, we've got them!" bellowed Harkann. "Cone out! Cone out!"

It was at this point that the Starwolves' unique ability to take the tremendous pressures of quick change of direction was brilliantly displayed. The metal of the flagship screeked in protest, and the blood drove again into Chane's skull, as the needle-shaped ship whirled away.

Every Varnan cruiser drove to its assigned position in one of the maneuvers that only Varnans could endure, and which they had practiced so many times that they almost do them in their sleep. With incredible quickness, the Starwolf ships formed into a gigantic conical pattern right in front of the onsweeping Qajar ships.

The Qajars could not react with the same swiftness, and their disorganized mass drove right into the giant cone. And the concentrated fire from all around them, the hail of missiles, shot half of them out of space.

"They're breaking!" cried Harkann. "Pour it on!"

Chane, loosing missiles as fast as he could get them off, saw the remaining Qajar ships turn wildly away, smashing clear of the cone of death. Three Varnan cruisers perished in head-on collisions.

And then the surviving Qajar vessels, no more than twenty-odd, were fleeing back in the direction of their world.

"After them!" ordered Harkann. "Three columns."

Chane saw things through a bloody haze, the pressure effect still clouding his vision.

It was only now, as they began the pursuit, that he realized that the probing finger of pain was still inside his skull.

XVIII

THIRTY STARWOLF SHIPS flew low over the surface of the shadowy planet Chlann. The other ships of the Varnan squadron were orbiting in detachments around the planet, wary lest the survivors of the Qajar fleet should return. But so far, none of them had returned.

Chane piloted the flagship now. He was supposed to be an expert on the Qajar world, he thought ironically. Fine. All he knew about it was the location of the city, the location of the treasure houses, and the fact that he had been clobbered real hard the last time he had been here.

"Stand by," he said. "I think we'll be coming up on it pretty quick."

It was dangerous flying starships this low over a planet. But the Varnans were used to it—it was part of their regular raid technique—and also they were used to danger.

"Looks like mines of some sort," said Vengant, peering down at the face of the planet as it whirled beneath them.

The primary of Chlann, the old, red, dying sun that was one of the few stars in this cluster with any life left in it at all, cast a dim, bloody light on the surface of the planet. Dark, stony, arid, lifeless, the world below appeared.

But Chane too had caught the glint of the ruddy light on great constructions of metal that rose out of the rock.

"Automated mines," he said. "I told you, this planet has enormous radite deposits, and that's where the Qajars got their wealth. There may be several cities, but I only know of the one, and it's coming up fast. Stand by."

Up over the horizon of the planet came a soft glow. He knew it at once, although he had only seen it in the tridims Eron had made.

The city of the Qajars. The glittering metal buildings, the domes and towers and minarets, all of them bathed in the blue glow that seemed to well up from the ground itself, a sourceless illumination that strangely enough did not seem to conflict or clash with the dusky light of the dying sun.

From the city, a bolt of white lightning shot up toward the advancing Varnan ships. Only it was not lightning at all, but a tremendous laser ray that ripped the air close in front of them. And then other laser batteries joined in, and their ships were flying into a forest of laser lightnings.

"Stunpower projectors on," said Harkann's hard voice, speaking through the communicator to the whole squadron.

A droning began back in the stern of the ship. At the same moment, two laser bolts caught a Varnan cruiser just behind them and sent it tumbling out of the sky.

"On," said the voice of their engineer.

The thirty Starwolf ships were flying in a broad line. And now from every one of them the fans of invisible powerful force swept down.

The force was just the same as that which was generated by the small hand-stunners they all wore in their belts. But instead of being generated by a small portable power pack, it was created by the mighty power units of the Starwolf ships, and it swept the whole terrain beneath them with a paralyzing, stunning force.

And as they flew over the streets of the glowing metal city, they saw the hurrying robed figures down there fall and lie still as the fans of force caught them.

It was the old Starwolf raiding technique. If you came in to a world using your missiles and laser full on, you could kill a lot of people but you would also destroy most of the loot you were after.

They went on over the city and the lasers that had been striking up at them from it fell still. A moment later, with a sense of immense relief, Chane felt the probing finger of pain in his head fade away.

Harkann uttered a rough oath. "So we got whoever was operating that damned pain ray! I'm only sorry we won't have time to hunt him out and kill him."

"*Look out!*" said Chane.

They were nearing the starport and from it there stabbed viciously an unexpected cluster of laser rays. Chane automatically spun into an evasive course, and the rays went by them.

Another Varnan ship was hit. Its shields were penetrated, and it tumbled downward. Harkann uttered a curse, and then they were past the starport, and its laser battery fell silent.

"Damn these people!" said Vengant. "I'd like to kill them, not just stun them."

"We haven't enough power for lethal, on the broad range we're using," said Harkann. "Otherwise, I agree with you."

Chane shrugged. "I don't mind their lasers, although I can't say I love them. But when I remember how they took my brain apart with that ray, I agree with you too."

"All right," said Harkann. "Come about and land on that starport. There may be some down there we didn't knock out, but we should be able to handle them."

He gave that order to the rest of their force, and then called up to the ships on watch in orbit. "Anything?"

"Not a thing," came the answer. "They've had the fight taken out of them and have landed and holed up somewhere."

"All right," said Harkann. "Let's go down and get the plunder."

They came down on the starport in a rush, and landed there in semidarkness under the black starless sky. They tumbled out of the ship fast, and all across the starport the big golden Varnans were coming out of the ships, the smell of loot in their nostrils and their eyes shining. And to Chane it was all as it had been since the first raid he had ever made, and what better life was there in the whole galaxy than to raid with the Starwolves?

"Break out the sleds," ordered Harkann. "And move!"

The starwolves prepared for their raids in a careful manner. When they hit a world they wanted to take what things they could there, and get away fast. For this the sleds were invaluable.

They were not really sleds. They were narrow, oblong flat hover-craft that nested together in a space just inside the hull of the ship. Chane helped pull them out and separate them.

Then Chane jumped onto the front end of one of them. He unfolded to an erect position the medium-heavy laser there. He opened the controls, and the sled rose several inches above the starport surface, its lifting-jets spuming up the dust underneath.

Vengant remained as ship-guard but the others now urged their sleds toward the city. Nobody among them waited to follow a leader; they raced across the starport in the semidarkness in any sort of order, shouting and laughing to each other.

Chane felt the high, fierce excitement he had always felt on these dashes. But he restrained it. He was now fast approaching the crisis of his whole struggle.

"This way!" bawled Harkann from his racing sled, pointing toward the blue radiance that rose beneath the dark, red-tinged sky.

They approached the smaller outer buildings of the city, gleaming metallically in the blue light. The air became perceptibly warmer as they entered the blue radiance. They whirled on toward the tall towers that glittered brightly in the center of the little city. And now Chane let his sled fall behind the others a bit without being too obvious about it.

They had the lasers on the fronts of the sleds, and wore their stunners in their belts, but there was no need to use them. The Qajars lay where they had fallen, in streets and buildings. They looked quite neat sleeping in their long robes, and the sleds racing over them cleared them and did not disturb them.

Chane wished he had time to look for the Qajar named Vlanalan, who had tortured Dilullo and Gwaath and himself.

But taking their stolen treasures will probably be revenge enough, he thought.

The Varnans poured into the metal towers. And quickly they started coming out, laughing and shouting and bringing the first of the loot.

Jewels, precious metals, priceless statuary, all the costly and superb treasures which the Qajars had had thieved for them from worlds far across the galaxy. The big Starwolves, their strength immense on this smaller planet, bundled these treasures together higgledy-piggledy into the carrying-nets they had brought and lifted it onto the sleds, and went back for more.

Chane unobtrusively steered his sled around the plaza toward the smaller, less-impressive looking tower he remembered from the tridim pictures. So far, it had been ignored. He ran up its steps, his heart beating rapidly, flung open the wide doors, and burst into the round, lofty room that he remembered.

It was the room of the tridim picture, with walls of black hung with silken black hangings, all of it designed to highlight the one thing that was in the room.

He looked at the Singing Suns, and now he heard their music.

138

XIX

A LONG TIME AGO on Earth a man named Plato had looked up at the planets of heaven and dreamed that in their stately movements they made each a glorious music.

Many centuries later, on a world far across the galaxy from Earth, a master artist had looked up at the stars and had the same dream. And because he was a master scientist as well as an artist, he had created the Singing Suns. His world was in decline and his arts lost and he himself long dead before the wider galactic life touched there, and nobody would ever create such a thing again.

And they do sing, thought Chane, standing with more of a look of awe on his dark, wild face than anyone had ever seen there.

There were forty of them, forty jewels that represented the forty mightiest stars. They had been synthetically created, but in their flashing splendor they made all natural gems look dull. Into each one had been built a tiny miniaturized generator that was fed by an almost unaging supply of transuranic fuel. And these generators powered the matrix of invisible force that held the Suns together, guided their movements, and produced the electronic sounds that made their music.

The jewels moved in an intricate pattern, a stardance that was too complicated at first to follow. Red, green, golden yellow, bright blue, they wove their unhurried ways in a design of mathematical perfection. The whole mobile of the Suns was only some four feet

139

in diameter, but its splendor to the eye was the fact that it was always changing, now one dark red star-jewel passing two golden ones, now an ethereal blue-white gliding above a greenish one.

And the jewels sang. From each one came its individual note of pure sound electronically produced, rising and falling in a lilting mode. And like the pattern of their movement, the pattern of their sound changed perpetually. Yet by the miracle that a master of both art and science had wrought, the changing web of sound was always music.

Chane stared, fascinated. No one who had roamed the starry universe could remain unmoved by this brilliant, changing, singing simulation of the great stars. There were the great suns that he knew well, the mighty red glare of Betelgeuse, the white blaze of Rigel, the golden splendor of Altair. It was as though he saw the whole changing, blazing galaxy in miniature, and the siren music of its components reinforced the sensation so that he seemed to fly as a disembodied spirit through the galactic spaces, rather than to stand looking at a mobile.

A Varnan shout not far outside the building startled Chane out of the spell. On a Starwolf raid, there was no time for dreaming!

And when they see what I've got, there'll be something like a Starwolf riot, he thought.

He hurried out and brought the sled right through the opening of the great double doors. Then he grasped the base of the mobile.

The thing was heavy, but his strength was quite sufficient on this lower-gravity world. He managed to tip and walk and work the base of the Singing Suns up onto the sled and fasten it securely. And even as he sweated at this task, the jewel-Suns only inches from his eyes continued their smooth, mazy motions and their music thrilled his ears.

When he was done he ripped down one of the black silk hangings from the wall and used it to cover the Singing Suns. Then he backed the sled out of the building and went away fast.

Under the blue radiance of the halo, the Qajar city was a strange scene. The Starwolves, intoxicated by the loot they were loading on the sleds, shouted and laughed at each other, big bawling golden figures gutting the treasures of the Qajars.

And the Qajars still lay sleeping in their robes, as the beauty they had plotted and stolen and tortured to obtain was taken away from them forever. Remembering the agony they had inflicted on him and his two comrades, Chane was fiercely glad.

He drove the sled out of the city at its highest speed, toward the starport. He passed out of the blue radiance and was again in the semidarkness beneath the mournful black sky. Now he met sleds returning from having loaded a first cargo of loot aboard ship, going back for more. Their drivers waved to him elatedly.

When he reached the starport and threaded his way between the little Varnan ships he saw loading still going on at some of them. With reckless speed, in the semidarkness, Chane drove on toward the flagship.

Outside the ship, as though waiting for him, stood two tall Varnan figures, dark in the shadows.

Vengant.

And Harkann.

Instantly Chane knew that there was going to be trouble. Harkann should not be here; he should be back in the city supervising the operation.

Chane stopped the sled and got off it. And Harkann said in a harsh voice, "I was curious, Chane. I found you'd slipped away and I wondered what it was you were after."

Chane shrugged. "The Council gave me the right to select one single treasure for myself—whatever I wanted. And why are you worried about that? Haven't I brought you to the greatest plunder Varna has taken for years?"

"The plunder is fine indeed," said Harkann. "So fine that I wondered why you would pass it by and go after something else. What have you got on the sled?"

Well, Chane thought, *it would have had to come to the pinch sooner or later, so it might as well be now.*

He reached forward with both hands and pulled the silken black hanging toward him.

Both Harkann and Vengant stared, astonished, at the glorious thing on the sled. "The Singing Suns," said Harkann slowly, and shook his head as though not believing what he saw. "They were broken up and sold, but here they are . . . for the second time in Varnan hands."

Chane, still holding the silken hanging idly, corrected him. "In my hand. I claim the Suns by Council right."

Harkann slowly turned his stunned gaze from the singing jewels to Chane. His face became passionate, his upslanting eyes flaming like embers.

"Oh, no," he said. "No outworld bastard is going to take this all for himself."

"The Council right—" began Chane, and Harkann raged, "The hell with the Council right. We Ranroi would have had your life anyway when we got back to Varna, and it might as well be now!"

Chane triggered his stunner. He had drawn it gently from his belt behind the black hanging he was holding, while the others were staring at the mobile in amazement and greed. The thing buzzed nastily and the force of it went through the cloth as easily as through air. Harkann and Vengant stiffened and toppled over.

Chane dropped the concealing cloth. He muttered to the two still forms, "I should have used it on lethal, but I've got enough feud with the Ranroi without that. Sleep for a while, my friends."

He glanced swiftly around. Some of the Varnan ships being loaded from the loot-piled sleds were not too far away, but in the noise and cheerful confusion and the semidarkness nobody seemed to have noticed.

He bent down and dragged Harkann and then Vengant some little distance from the ship and threw the black hanging over them.

The air lock doors of the ship were open, and they were very wide doors, wide enough to admit a sled. When the Starwolves departed a planet with a load of loot they wanted to depart in a hurry. Chane ran the sled up the gangway and into the ship and maneuvered it to the rear of the main compartment. There were clamps there to lock sleds fast, and in a moment he had his cargo secured. The Suns glittered and sang and wove their dance serenely.

Chane jumped to the pilot chair, hit the lever that sealed all locks, and got the power unit started. When the power unit had built to a barely sufficient level, Chane took the little ship off in a steep climb.

As he shot toward the starless sky he looked down and could see startled faces turned up to him. It would not be long, he thought, before somebody stumbled over Harkann and Vengant. But it would take quite a time to bring them around, time enough, he hoped, to get away with the Suns.

A sudden wild elation filled him as he sent the little ship arrowing out headlong from dark Chlann. He had snatched the Singing Suns away from the damned Qajars and from Harkann both.

He had not planned at all to do it this way. He had supposed that he would have no choice but to go back to Varna with Harkann, and then try to slip away with the Suns before the Ranroi could finish him off. He had never had the slightest intention of going through single combats with one after another of the Ranroi until inevitably they got him. He considered that too damned unfair, when there were hundreds of them and only one of him.

But Harkann had changed the plan by his sudden access of rage, and Chane like a good Starwolf, had changed his tactics in mid-leap.

Fine, he thought. *This is much better . . . so far. But what if they track me?*

That was a problem he would have to face, but not now. His first job was to get out of the dark, crowded cluster and into overdrive.

He headed the ship through the clutter of ashen suns and stony black planets, toward the Spur but not toward Rith. Instead, he laid his course for Varna.

They would be ranging him, back there on Chlann, wondering why the devil a Varnan ship had taken off prematurely, and where it was going. He had better try to deceive them as to his course, though he knew in his heart that no Starwolf would fall for such a clumsy trick. At the moment, it was the only one he could think of.

It was dangerous to go into overdrive too near to a

celestial body of any size. It had been done, but not very often. More times than not, the gravitic field had flawed the overdrive reaction and made wreckage out of the ship.

Chane was always willing to take chances but it did not seem to him that there was any real need to risk suicide. He urged the ship to its highest speed, thinking as he looked at the view-port that he never wanted to see this cursed little clutch of dead suns and mournful planets again.

He broke clear of the cluster at last, and now in the distance ahead stretched the immense coast of tarnished fire that was the Argo Spur. When he was at a marginally safe distance from the cluster, he set up the overdrive controls.

Before switching on he looked back at the rear range screen. There were four blips showing, and he knew then that he had overestimated the time it would take to bring Harkann back to consciousness.

"That's what I get for playing it soft like John is always telling me," he muttered. "I should have used lethal."

The pursuers were after him.

XX

IT WAS a dead, dark, airless world, infinitely desolate and useless, but it was a hiding place. And Chane was hiding.

He had got well inside the Spur when he decided that he had best go to ground. He knew the bitterness and rage with which Harkann and his Ranroi would sweep and quarter after him, waiting for the time when he would have to come out of overdrive, when they could spot him and pounce.

He could not fight four cruisers, or one cruiser. He was only one man, not a crew, and while he could keep the ship going he could not possibly fly it and fight it both. A hiding place was his best chance, and this dead planet of a giant red star looked like the best one he could find in time.

There were no telltale blips on his screen as yet. But he knew better than to linger.

He had dropped out of overdrive on the back side of the dead planet, so that the mass of the world itself served as a screen against their radar. Then he began a quick and frantic search for metal deposits. When the analyzer showed him one of a size and content to meet his needs, he landed the ship at once.

It was a hazardous landing, in the bottom of a narrow gully between glistening rock walls. The ship took a banging, but endured. Chane got into his suit and helmet, cracked the lock and clambered out. Climbing up the side of the rock wall, he used one of the portable lasers he had brought to dislodge a shower of small fragments and he hoped that he was not going to dislodge a big boulder that would crash down and do an evil to the ship. He did not. He played the laser with skill, and presently the upper part of the ship's hull was dusted thickly with particles of rock debris.

It was a pretty faulty protective coloration, Chane thought, but it would have to do. The debris, containing heavy metal deposits, should blend the ship more or less indistinguishably into the background. The Ranroi would do a search sweep with their analyzers, but Varnan analyzers were not fine scientific instruments; they were, rather, simple affairs designed to detect ambushed ships and the like. With luck, they would simply note an area of metal-bearing rock and go on.

With luck. . . .

Sitting in his camouflaged ship and watching the screen, Chane grinned to himself. Luck. "If we have luck they'll go away." That was what Nimurun had said years ago when their Starwolf party had raided the Pleiades and nearly been caught, and they had had to hide their ships in the ghastly metal ruins of a war-destroyed world. Well, they had had luck that time, and all he could do now was hope it would repeat, and in the meantime drink some of the Varnan wine and watch the screen.

Nothing, yet. But he was sure they would be along. They could be very patient, very thorough in their search.

He turned and considered the Singing Suns. Here in the confines of the ship their music was louder, but still soft. It changed and changed in infinite permutations of melodic phrases, always singing of the glory of the great suns, the majesty and burning splendor of the mighty stars that lorded space.

And the Suns moved in their endless glittering mazy dance, and when he looked at them long enough it was as it had been when he first saw them on Chlann: he seemed to be drawn among them and they became, not singing jewels, but flaming giants whose mighty star-song filled the whole of space.

An hypnotic effect? He did not think so. The Suns had no need for such tricks as hypnotism. Their beauty of sight and sound held one imprisoned in a dream.

He had better not get too imprisoned, he thought, and turned to look again at the screen.

He tensed sharply. Two blips moved across it, two

ships orbiting this dead world at high speed, moving in the familiar search-sweep pattern. Chane knew that their analyzers, tuned to detect metal, would be probing with broad fans of force, seeking a metal ship on the desolate rock.

The blips came around fast and Chane whispered, "Nothing down here but a metal outcrop, boys. Go right on."

They did. Had the metal outcrop fooled them, or would they come down to investigate?

The minutes went by. The Suns sang softly, of cosmic beauty and strength, of beginnings and endings, of the life of stars which men can never know.

The two blips came on again. They were continuing the search pattern southward. They were not coming down. Chane exhaled pent-up breath.

He continued to watch as they completed their sweep of the planet. Finally the two blips left the screen entirely. They had gone.

Chane did nothing. He continued to sit there and pour himself the golden wine and listen to the singing of the Suns.

He was not through with the Ranroi yet.

Harkann and his little squadron would shake out this whole part of the Spur before they left. That was certain. For Harkann would not want to go back to Varna and admit that his clan-enemy the damned Earthman had foxed him, used his mission as a cat's-paw to take the Singing Suns, and gone off with them in Harkann's own ship. Even though the raid would have brought home plunder rich beyond even Starwolf dreams, Harkann would not want to face that.

How Berkt would laugh if he heard that, thought Chane. *How all Varna would laugh!*

But the laughter would never come if Harkann could prevent it. He and his Ranroi ships would hang to the search like grim death.

Should he leave this planet, try to slip away before the search swung back? Chane thought not. It was exactly what they were looking for; this preliminary sweep was designed to flush him out, urge him to run so that he could be spotted and chased. He had made his gamble when he hid here, and he would push that bet all the way.

He drank, and ate, and slept, and waited. He did not once go outside the ship. Nothing must be disturbed in any way.

Days went by before two blips again came onto the screen. The two ships made exactly the same search-sweep over the planet as before. And Chane knew that the analyzers would be probing again while their little tape-banks chattered through Comparison. If one small object did not correspond exactly with the record of the first sweep, the ship would land and investigate.

The two ships finished their search and went away again. But still Chane made no move. A section of the Spur was a big place to search, and the Ranroi would likely be around for quite some time yet.

Chane hated waiting and doing nothing; all Star-wolves hated that. But they could be very good at it when they had to, for there were times in their dangerous trade when it was necessary.

The Suns sang on. It seemed to him, as he watched and listened day after day, that the rising and falling music spoke words, not faulty words such as humans use, but the pure and perfect language of stars.

What did stars talk about, in that silver-singing speech? Of the birth of the universe, when they first exploded into being? Of the mighty rivers of force that ran between them, of the darkening and dying of old comrades, of the dreadful and glorious fate of novae, of the thin, far-off messages that came from brother giants remote across the intergalactic void?

Chane dreamed of these things, but this time he did not let his dreaming interrupt his careful watch on the screens. And there came a time when he saw five faint and distant blips moving away in the direction of Varna.

Chane laughed. "So you finally gave it up, Harkann? I'll gamble that your crews made you do it."

Chane knew the Starwolves, and he knew how it would be with those crews, how eager they would be to get back to Varna and celebrate one of the richest raids in history, and to hell with Ranroi vengeance and Harkann's private feud until after we've had a time!

He waited for a safe interval and then got busy. He put on the suit and helmet, unclamped the sled which bore the Suns, and maneuvered it out through the big air lock into the vacuum outside.

The fierce glare of the red giant illuminated the floor of the narrow rock valley. Chane drove the sled along the valley, mile after mile, until he found the place he wanted.

It was a deep cave in the base of one of the enclosing cliffs. It could not have been formed by erosion —this world had never had an atmosphere from its looks—but bursting gases when the planet was formed had created this bubble. High above it on the steep cliff-face was a place where the rock bulged outward.

Chane drove the sled deep into the cave. He took the Singing Suns off the sled and set them on the rock. In the darkness here they still gleamed with supernal beauty, but in the soundless vacuum he could not hear them.

He left the Suns there and backed the sled outside. Then with the laser mounted on the sled he attacked the bulge of rock high above on the cliff. The laser flashed and flashed, quite silently, cutting deep. Finally a section of the cliff tumbled down and effectively sealed the entrance to the cave.

Chane made careful note of the exact location and then turned the sled back toward the ship.

When he was ready he took the ship off with a bold rush. It was an almost suicidal risk to take off from a cramped place like this valley, and he wanted to make it fast or not at all.

He made it. He came up off the dead planet and swept past the glaring red sun, laying his course for Rith.

XXI

STORM was sweeping across the night side of Rith where the little capital of Eron lay. Chane had counted on the frequency of the storms here, and he had not brought his ship toward the planet until he was sure another of the interminable tempests was raging.

The ships of the Starwolves were unmistakable because of their small, needle-like shape that had been designed to endure the sudden turns that gave the Varnans their big advantage in space. And when a Starwolf ship arrived at any planet other than Varna it would pretty surely be met by a hail of missiles. Chane had had experience with the way the great thunderstorms of Rith played the devil with radar and

151

scanners, and he was hoping to get down on the starport without being scanned.

He got the ship down all right, and the solid downpour of water prevented visual observation. But also his own instruments being aborted led to his making such a bad landing that he was glad no one had seen it.

He worked very fast now, before the storm should cease. He set up the automatic controls so that in three minutes the ship would take off on a course laid for Varna, with the automatic trips set to detour around all celestial obstacles. He was damned if he was going to let a Varnan ship and its secrets fall into enemy hands.

He was grinning as he cracked the lock and started out of the ship.

"How sheepish Harkann will be if his ship comes wandering home empty-handed after him!"

The rain smashing in his face took the laughter out of him. He started struggling through the hellish downpour, and he only heard in a muffled way when the ship he had just left took off. He hoped he could make it to one of the starport administration buildings before he was flattened.

Two hours later, Chane sat in the big cold barny room he had burglarized not too long before. Two of the runty red guards watched him. He thought they must be the same two he had knocked out and tied up, the muderous way they watched him.

Eron and Dilullo came in. Dilullo gave Chane a sour look that had no warmth in it.

"So, we've got you back again, have we?" he said.

"Thanks for the welcome, John," said Chane. "From the way you look, and from the fact you've recovered your usual sunny temper, I take it you're normal again."

Eron had folded his arms and was glaring at Chane in what was intended to be a crushing manner. But when Chane did not look at him, the little red king suddenly roared, "You stole one of my scout-ships! Where is it?"

Chane smiled at him. "It's far away. I don't think you'll ever see it again."

Eron began to curse. "The men at the starport said they thought a ship landed you and then took off again. What kind of ship?"

"A Starwolf ship," said Chane.

That made Eron's eyes pop. But Dilullo looked at Chane and for this once, at least, a warm light came into his eyes.

"Chane, then you went home to Varna? And you got back alive? How was it?"

"It was wonderful, and it was dangerous," said Chane, "and I'm damned glad I did it."

Eron broke in, raging. "You Mercs have been nothing but bad luck to me since you came here. This settles it—when the Qajars demand you you'll all be turned over to them. I don't care if they put you over a slow fire."

"Relax, Eron," said Chane. "It will be a long time before the Qajars bother you or anyone else. Those nice, crazy, torture-happy, beauty-loving people have been most thoroughly smashed, and their world has been most thoroughly looted, and I don't think anyone will hear anything from them for a long time."

"Smashed? With their defenses?" cried Eron. "Lies, lies. Who could do that?"

"The Starwolves did it," said Chane, and his teeth flashed. "And I led them there." And he turned to Dilullo and said, "We didn't really kill hardly anybody there, John, but we did strip them clean, and that pays them off for the fun they had with us."

"Those treasures!" cried Eron. "And the Singing Suns? What became of them?"

"I got them," said Chane.

Eron began to shout again. "Lies, lies! You had nothing, nothing at all, when you landed on Rith."

Chane nodded. "Of course. Do you think I would bring the Singing Suns here, so you could grab hold of them and then boot our behinds off this world? Little man, I'm not that foolish!"

Eron stared at him, and then burst into a bellow of laughter.

"I knew," he told Chane, "the first time I saw you that you were a bastard of a Starwolf!" He came up to Chane and grabbed his arm. "So you did it, eh? Tell me how?"

Chane told him. Dilullo, listening, watched Chane's face and said nothing. But Eron again and again rocked with crowing laughter.

"Wonderful, wonderful!" he cried. "But where, actually, are the Singing Suns?"

Chane patted him on the shoulder. "You're a nice little king, Eron, and I rather like you in a way, but please don't insult me with questions like that."

Eron shrugged. "Well, I can see your point. It happens that I'm the soul of honor, but you couldn't be expected to know that. Just tell me how and when you'll turn over my half of the two million credits' reward. That was our deal, you remember."

"That *was* our deal," Chane said. "But if you recall, that deal went sour when your information and your ship didn't get us anywhere near the Suns. The deal was off, and you were going to feed us to the Qajars if they wanted us. I broke loose, and now we have a new deal."

"What kind of deal?" asked Eron, looking black but crafty.

Chane smiled. "I'm generous to a fault. When the Suns are taken back to Achernar, you get one-tenth of the reward."

"One-tenth?" Eron began to curse in his native language and Chane said, "Put it into galacto, if you want me to get it."

Eron lost his good humor completely. His face became stony and dangerous. He glared at Chane.

"All right," he said. "I've tried to be nice about this. But you've hidden the Suns somewhere and now you come swaggering in here and think you've got the upper hand. You forget that I've got you right in the hollow of my hand. Just a few hours of Rith working-over and you'll be babbling all you know about the Suns."

Chane shook his head. "It won't work. Nobody ever got anything out of a Starwolf by torture. And you know why? It's because, to protect the secrets of Varna, every Starwolf who goes on a raid has a drug capsule under his skin. All I have to do is press my skin in a certain place and then my body is completely anesthetized and you could carve on me all day and I'd never feel it."

Eron stared at him, startled. "Is that true?"

"No," said Chane. "It's a great big bluff and a lie."

And he broke into laughter, and Eron roared with him.

Dilullo sprang up from his chair. "God save me from

getting into any deals with people who think everything's funny."

"Relax, John," said Chane. "I think Eron and I understand each other."

"Sure we do," said Eron, going hail-fellow-well-met again. He clapped Chane on the back. "Bluff or no bluff, nobody's ever made a Starwolf talk. Let's sit down and bargain this like gentlemen."

They sat down at a table. Eron called for flagons of the strong Rith liquor, and then more flagons. Dilullo drank it, but looked like a thundercloud.

As time went on it was evident that Eron was trying to get them very drunk. But it was not working very well. Dilullo would not drink that much. Chane tossed it off goblet for goblet with Eron, but he had the stronger head. He kept shaking it at Eron and turning boredly away to watch the decorative dancing-girls who had appeared.

"Fifteen percent," Chane said finally. "The absolute last offer. Look, better fifteen percent of something than nothing."

"Twenty-five, or I'll have you all lasered before morning," said Eron.

"Not one percent, not one hundredth of a percent more," Chane told him, and poured more liquor into the goblets.

"Look," interrupted Dilullo, "my head aches, my rump aches, I'm sick of all this haggling." He said to Eron, "Twenty percent, or let the whole thing go."

Eron considered. "Four hundred thousand credits. Well . . ." He suddenly added, "But I have the price of my stolen scout ship as well."

Dilullo said, "All right, that seems fair enough. How do you want it?"

"Not in galactic credits," Eron said. "We don't trust that currency in the Spur. Bring it in jewels. I'll give you a list."

He added, "One more thing. Just so you remember to come back again with my share, I'll keep your friend Chane here with me. He's a good drinking companion."

"I was pretty sure," said Chane, "you would insist on some such little condition. All right." He looked at Dilullo. "I'll tell you in the morning where the Suns are hidden, so you can take them to Achernar."

"By all means wait until morning to tell me," said Dilullo. "You're in no condition to tell anyone directions to anything right now."

In the morning, after Chane had given Dilullo the location of the Suns on the dead world of the red giant, the Mercs took off in their ship.

Chane remained. He was a guest, an honored guest, and little red men with lasers watched him day and night.

He did not find it unpleasant. Eron insisted on trying to drink him down every night, but each time it was Eron who ended up with his head on the table. Nearly every night, after that, Chane tried to make a connection with one of the dancing-girls, who were attracted but also afraid.

The days, the weeks, the perpetual storms went by, and Chane was beginning to get just a little bored by the time the Merc ship called in for a landing.

Dilullo alone came from the starport to the pawky palace and put a package down in front of Eron.

"There it is," he said. "You can look the jewels over if you like."

Eron told him, "I can tell when I can trust a man, so there's no need. However, since you suggest it . . ."

The hours went by while the jewels were examined by Eron's experts. Then the little red monarch exclaimed, "All there."

"I may add," Dilullo said, "that there are no jewels, no credits, nor anything else of value on our ship, so that it will not profit you to detain us."

"As if I would!" said Eron. He clapped Chane on the back. "Well, I'll miss you, Starwolf. Good luck."

"Good luck to you, Eron," said Chane. "You just might find some good pickings left at Chlann, now that the Qajar defenses have been broken."

"I hate to break up these affectionate leavetakings between fellow robbers," grated Dilullo. "But if you don't *mind* . . ."

He and Chane, at the starport, walked out together toward the waiting Merc ship.

"So you went to Varna, and you raided again with the Starwolves," said Dilullo. "How was your homecoming, Chane? The same as it was with me, at Brindisi?"

Chane considered. "Not quite the same. Most of the people I knew were still there. But . . . I can't go back there again."

"Well," said Dilullo, "you're younger than I am, and that's what made the difference."

Then he added, "The devil with all this nostalgia. A starman's home is space. Let's go."

They went.